Acclaim for Kean Soo's

"A simply wonderful tale of friendship and whimsy,
masterfully constructed with depth and moxie."
—Kirkus Reviews

"Sophisticated and thoughtful,
this comic also has plenty of child appeal."
—School Library Journal

"I'm addicted to Jellaby! Kean Soo's
storytelling is irresistable."
—Scott McCloud, author of Understanding Comics

"Jellaby will win your heart."
—Jeff Smith, creator of Bone

Eisner Award nominee
for Best Digital Comic

Joe Shuster Award winner
for Best Comic for Kids

JELLABY

The Lost Monster

Kean Soo

CAPSTONE
www.capstoneyoungreaders.com

Acknowledgements:
Special thanks to Calista Brill, Roberta Pressel,
Judy Hansen, Hope Larson, David & Nicolas Seigneret, Ben
Hu, Jason Turner, Clio Chiang, Kazu Kibuishi, and of course,
all my friends and family for their love and support
over the years. A very special thank-you to the Canada
Council for the Arts for their support of this work.

Jellaby is published by Capstone
1710 Roe Crest Drive
North Mankato, Minnesota 56003
www.capstoneyoungreaders.com

Text © Kean Soo 2014
Illustrations © Kean Soo 2014

Cataloging-in-Publication Data is available on the Library of Congress website.
ISBN: 978-1-4342-6420-6 (paperback)

Summary:
After moving to a new neighborhood, ten-year-old Portia Bennett
finds a new best friend -- a huge purple monster behind her house!
Convinced the sweet, silent creature is lost, Portia decides to help
Jellaby find his way home. Together, these new friends embark
on a mysterious and extraordinary adventure.

Cover Design: Kean Soo & Kazu Kibuishi

Printed in China.
062014
008297R

Foreword

When Kean asked me to help him redesign the cover for this new edition of *Jellaby* you are now holding in your hands, I accepted enthusiastically, of course. Kean and I actually go way back. He was one of the first friends I made through email exchanges while drawing webcomics. At the time, Kean was drawing one of the best journal comics on the Internet. It was often highlighted by Scott McCloud -- our mentor and the driving inspiration for the creation of webcomics. During the long drawing sessions that often lasted through the night, Kean and I would chat and encourage each other as we worked.

It was a great, formative time in our careers. Soon, we collaborated on the *Flight* anthology, and Kean was one of its first contributors, but he also served as its assistant editor, having been there from the moment of its creation. He is uncle to my kids, he is a close friend, and his work is an inspiration to all those who know him.

We often bonded over a shared love of the work of Hayao Miyazaki, Bill Watterson, Jeff Smith, Osamu Tezuka, and other masters. This love is something I feel is clearly evident in the pages of *Jellaby*. Kean is working to carry on the tradition of great comic strip storytelling, and he does it while exhibiting the warmth and empathy that he himself carries with him. This is the quiet, introspective, cautious, and caring Kean. These are the first steps in a promising career of a great modern cartoonist. Someday people will also see the goofy, jolly, belly-laughing Kean that so many of us know in person. When the poop jokes start flying, I have a feeling that the readers will be in for quite a wild ride.

In the meantime, I encourage everyone to read and enjoy this wonderful story, as I think it is one of the greatest comics written for all ages, and I hope *Jellaby* continues to walk, or shuffle, among us for many years to come.

~ Kazu Kibuishi,
creator of the bestselling
Amulet series

CHAPTER ONE

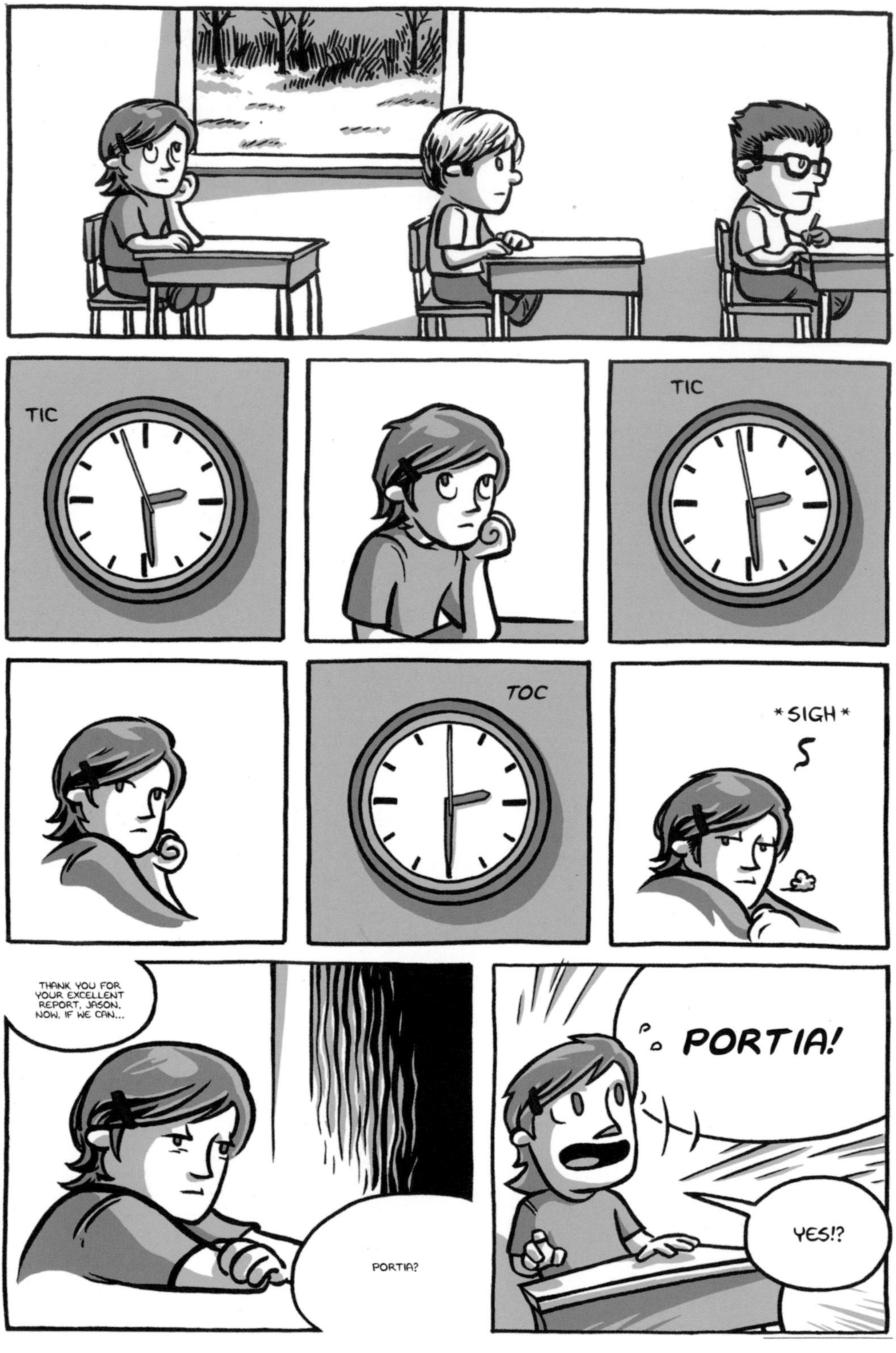

TIC
TIC
TOC
SIGH
THANK YOU FOR YOUR EXCELLENT REPORT, JASON. NOW, IF WE CAN...
PORTIA?
PORTIA!
YES!?

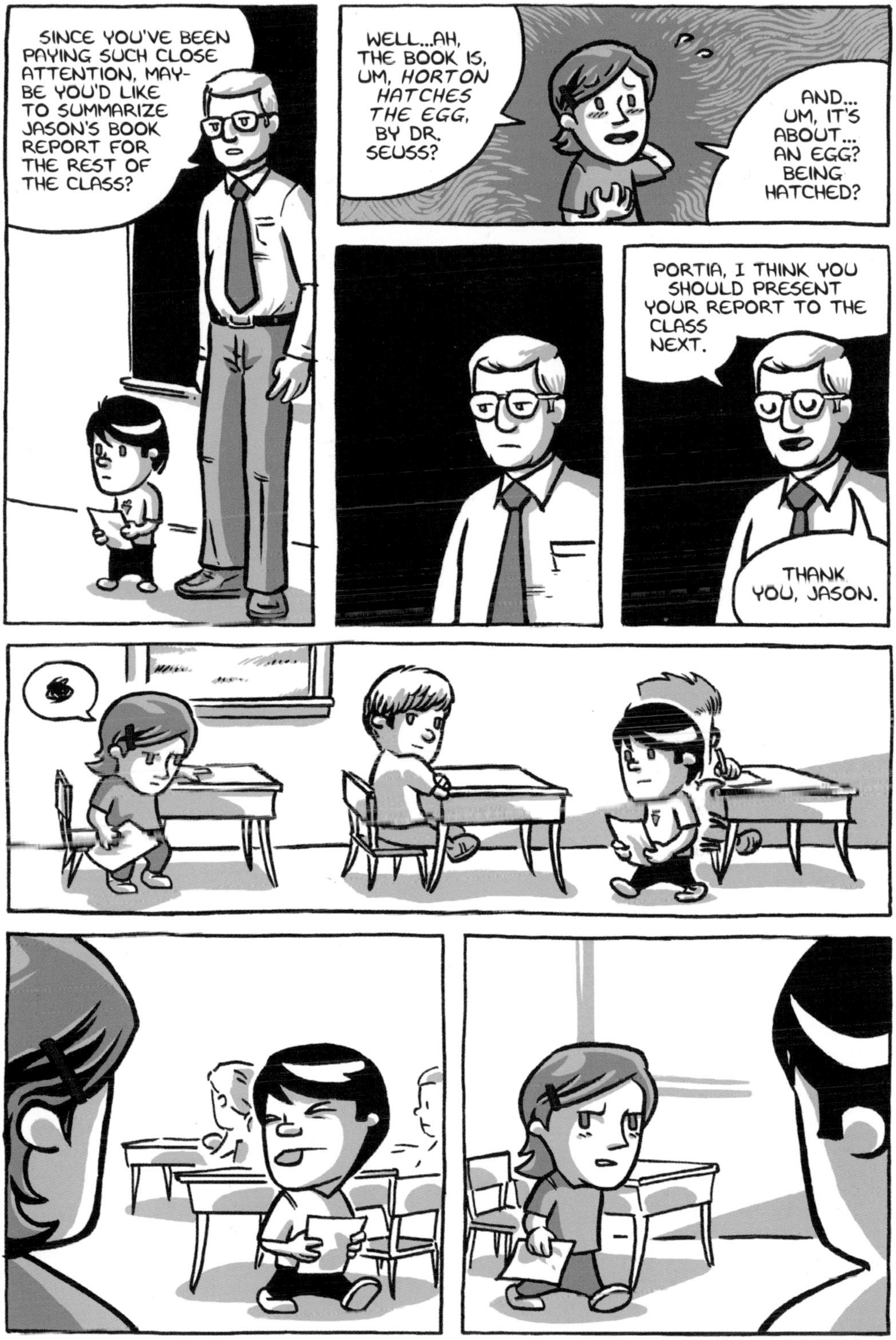
SINCE YOU'VE BEEN PAYING SUCH CLOSE ATTENTION, MAYBE YOU'D LIKE TO SUMMARIZE JASON'S BOOK REPORT FOR THE REST OF THE CLASS?
WELL...AH, THE BOOK IS, UM, *HORTON HATCHES THE EGG*, BY DR. SEUSS?
AND... UM, IT'S ABOUT... AN EGG? BEING HATCHED?
PORTIA, I THINK YOU SHOULD PRESENT YOUR REPORT TO THE CLASS NEXT.
THANK YOU, JASON.

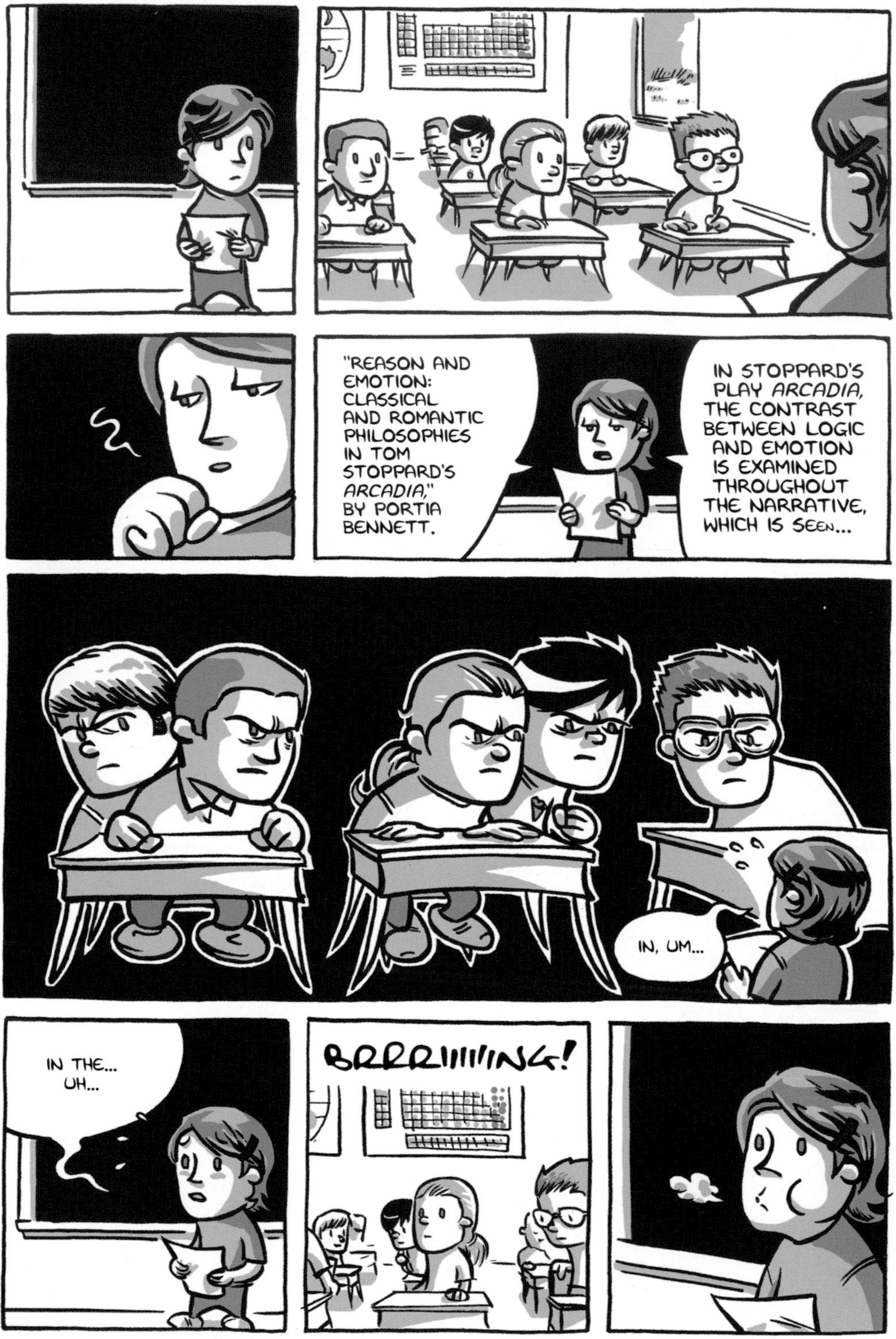
"REASON AND EMOTION: CLASSICAL AND ROMANTIC PHILOSOPHIES IN TOM STOPPARD'S *ARCADIA*," BY PORTIA BENNETT.
IN STOPPARD'S PLAY *ARCADIA*, THE CONTRAST BETWEEN LOGIC AND EMOTION IS EXAMINED THROUGHOUT THE NARRATIVE, WHICH IS SEEN...
IN, UM...
IN THE... UH...
BRRRIIIIIING!

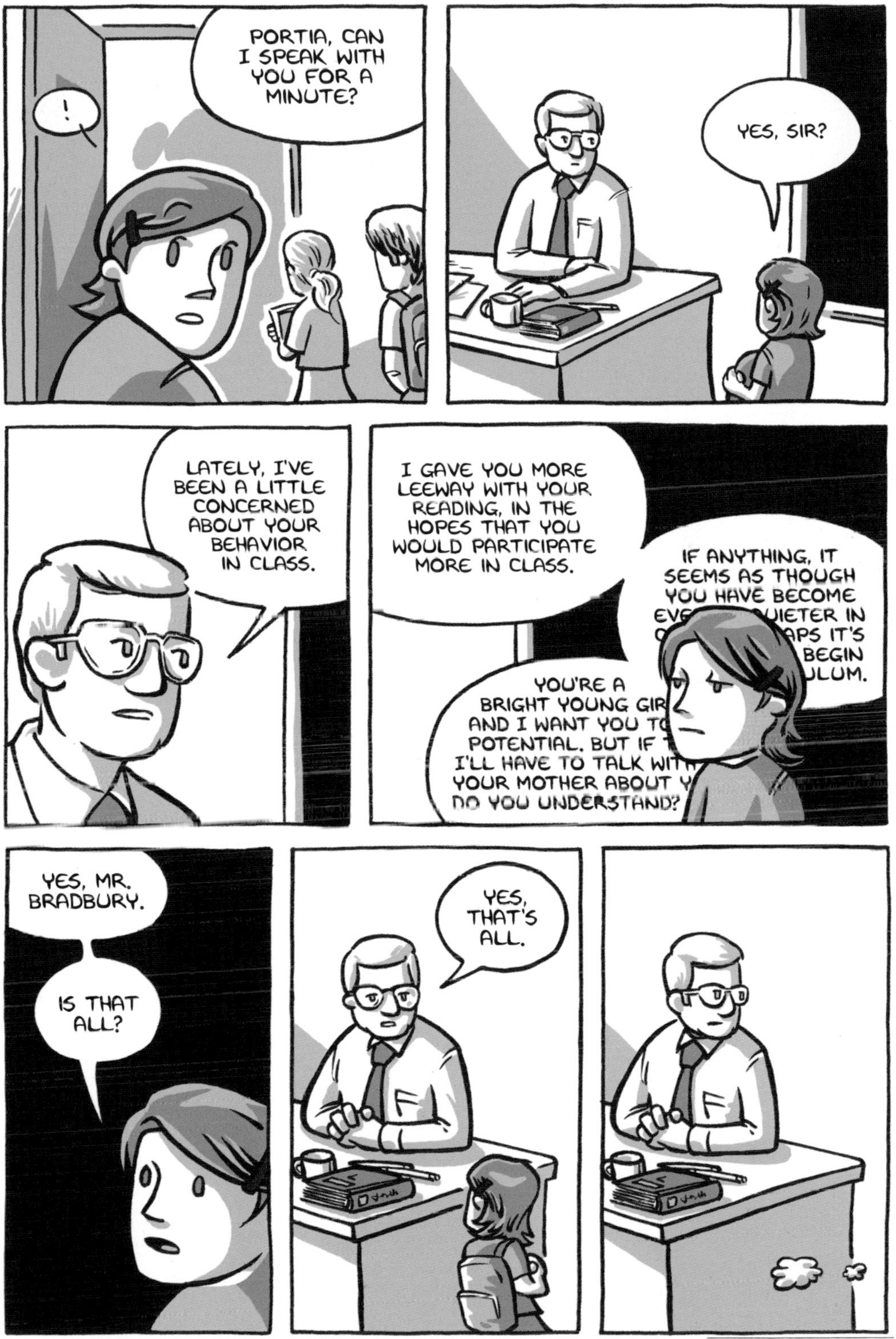
PORTIA, CAN I SPEAK WITH YOU FOR A MINUTE?
!
YES, SIR?
LATELY, I'VE BEEN A LITTLE CONCERNED ABOUT YOUR BEHAVIOR IN CLASS.
I GAVE YOU MORE LEEWAY WITH YOUR READING, IN THE HOPES THAT YOU WOULD PARTICIPATE MORE IN CLASS.
IF ANYTHING, IT SEEMS AS THOUGH YOU HAVE BECOME
YOU'RE A BRIGHT YOUNG GIR
YES, MR. BRADBURY.
IS THAT ALL?
YES, THAT'S ALL.

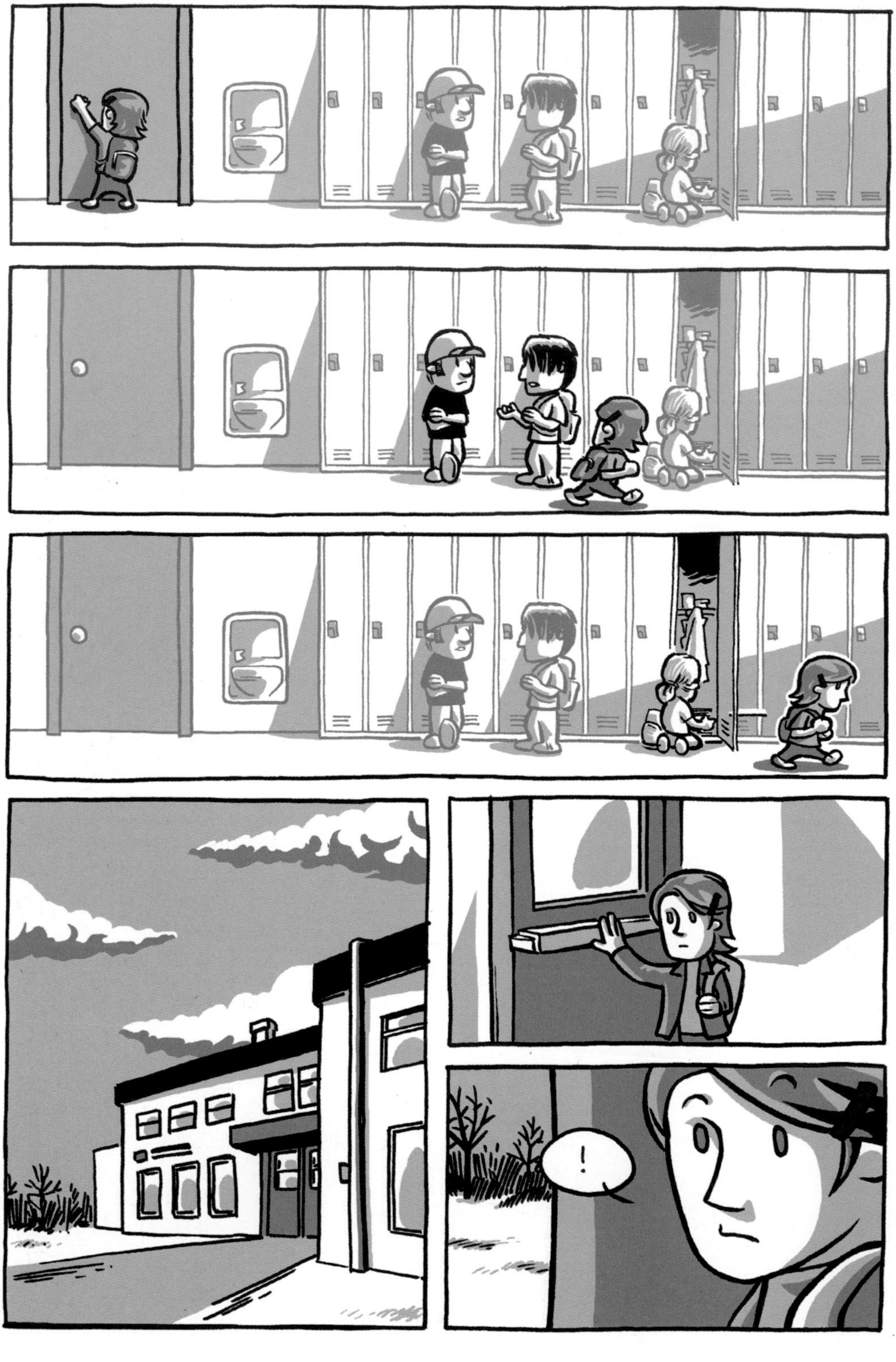
!

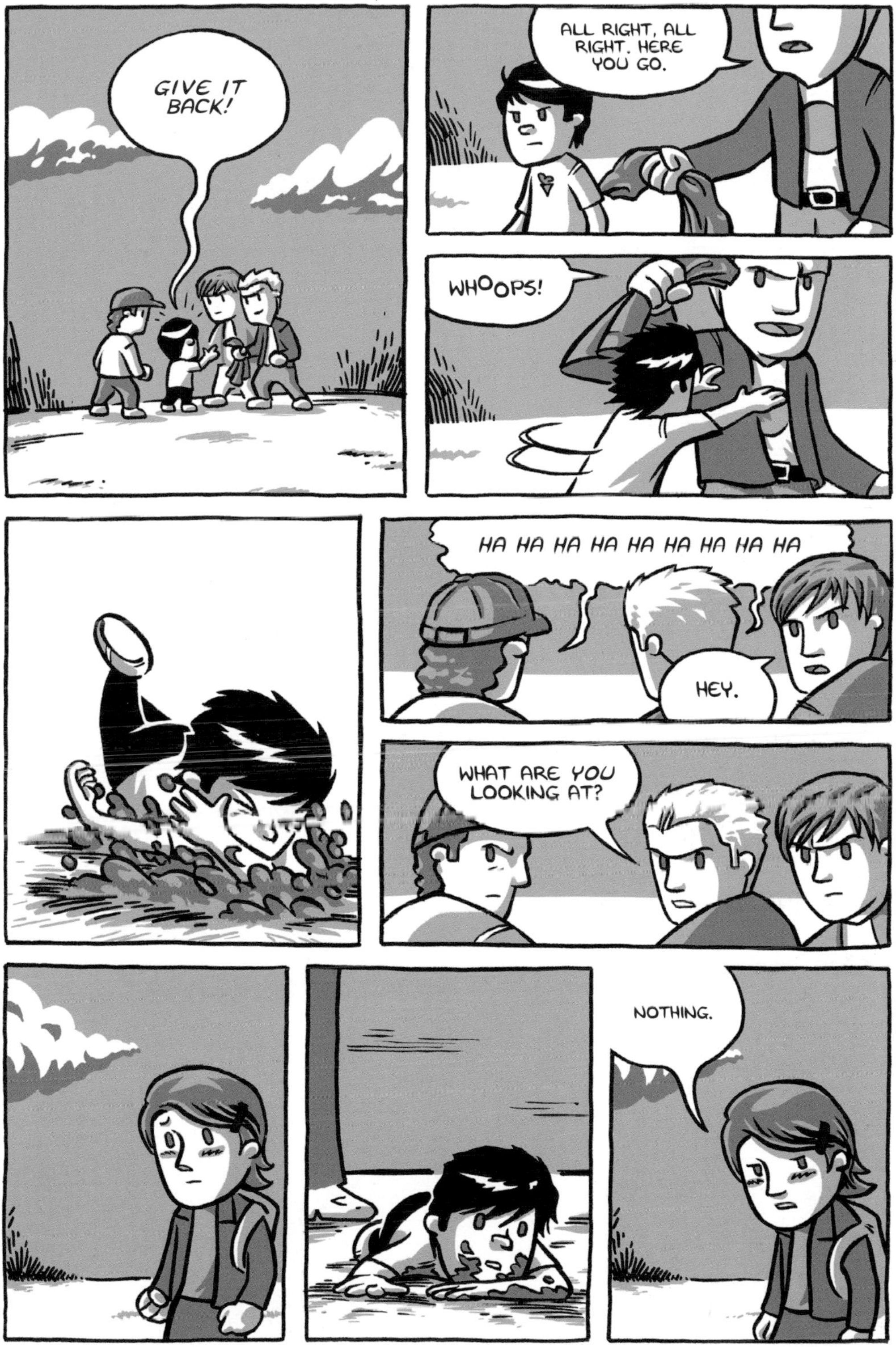
GIVE IT BACK!
ALL RIGHT, ALL RIGHT. HERE YOU GO.
WHOOPS!
HA HA HA HA HA HA HA HA HA
HEY.
WHAT ARE YOU LOOKING AT?
NOTHING.

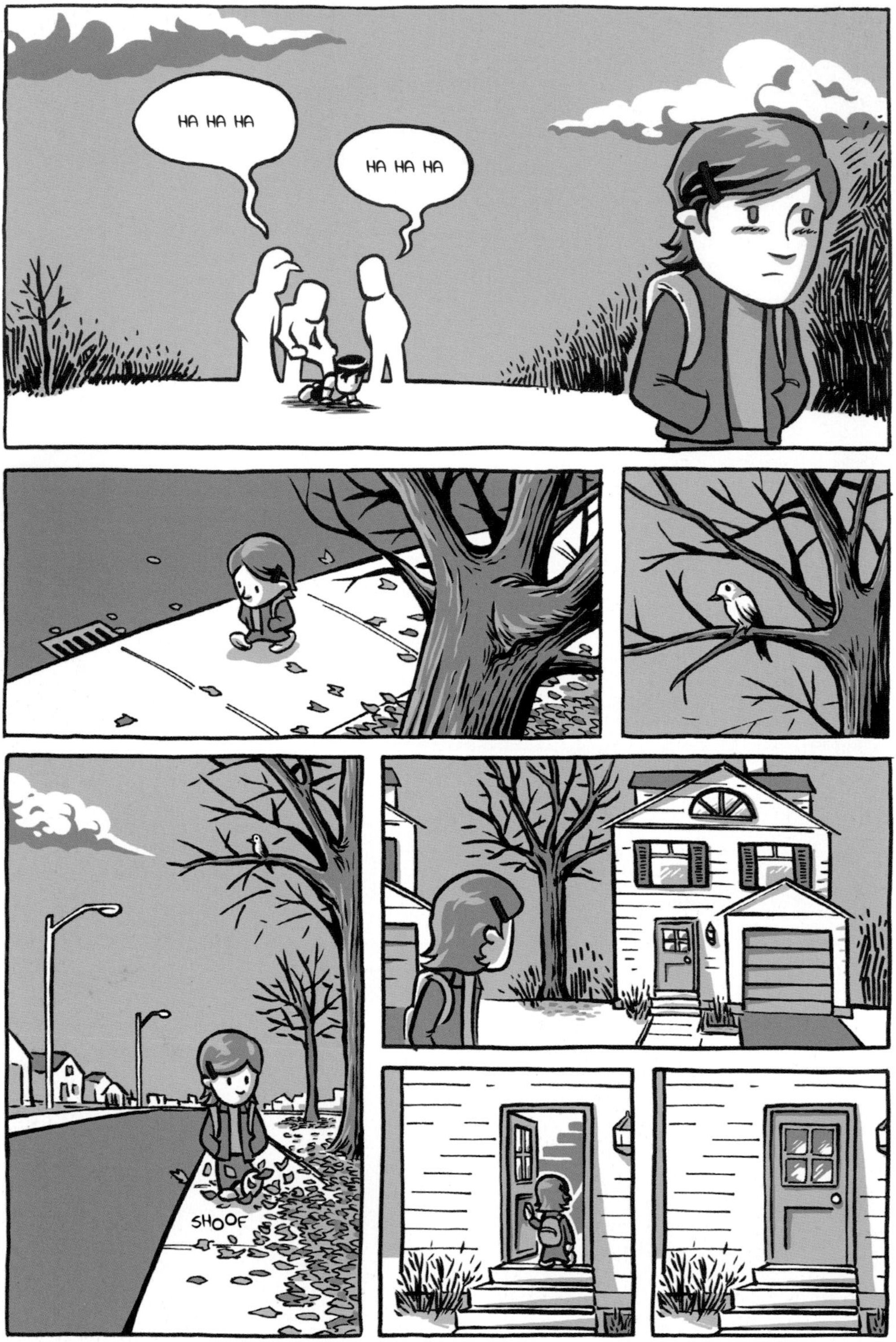
HA HA HA
HA HA HA
SHOOF

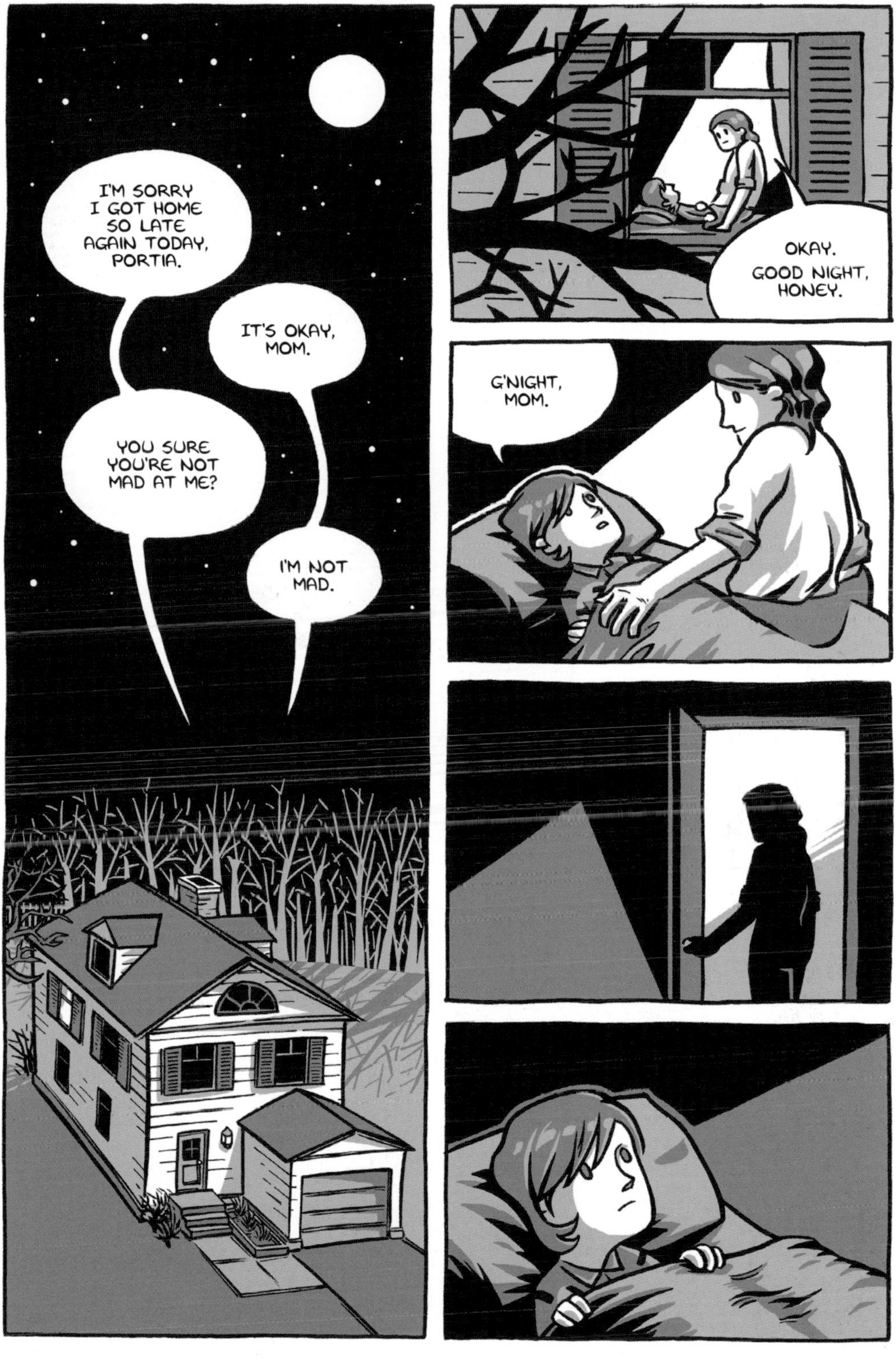
I'M SORRY I GOT HOME SO LATE AGAIN TODAY, PORTIA.
IT'S OKAY, MOM.
YOU SURE YOU'RE NOT MAD AT ME?
I'M NOT MAD.
OKAY. GOOD NIGHT, HONEY.
G'NIGHT, MOM.

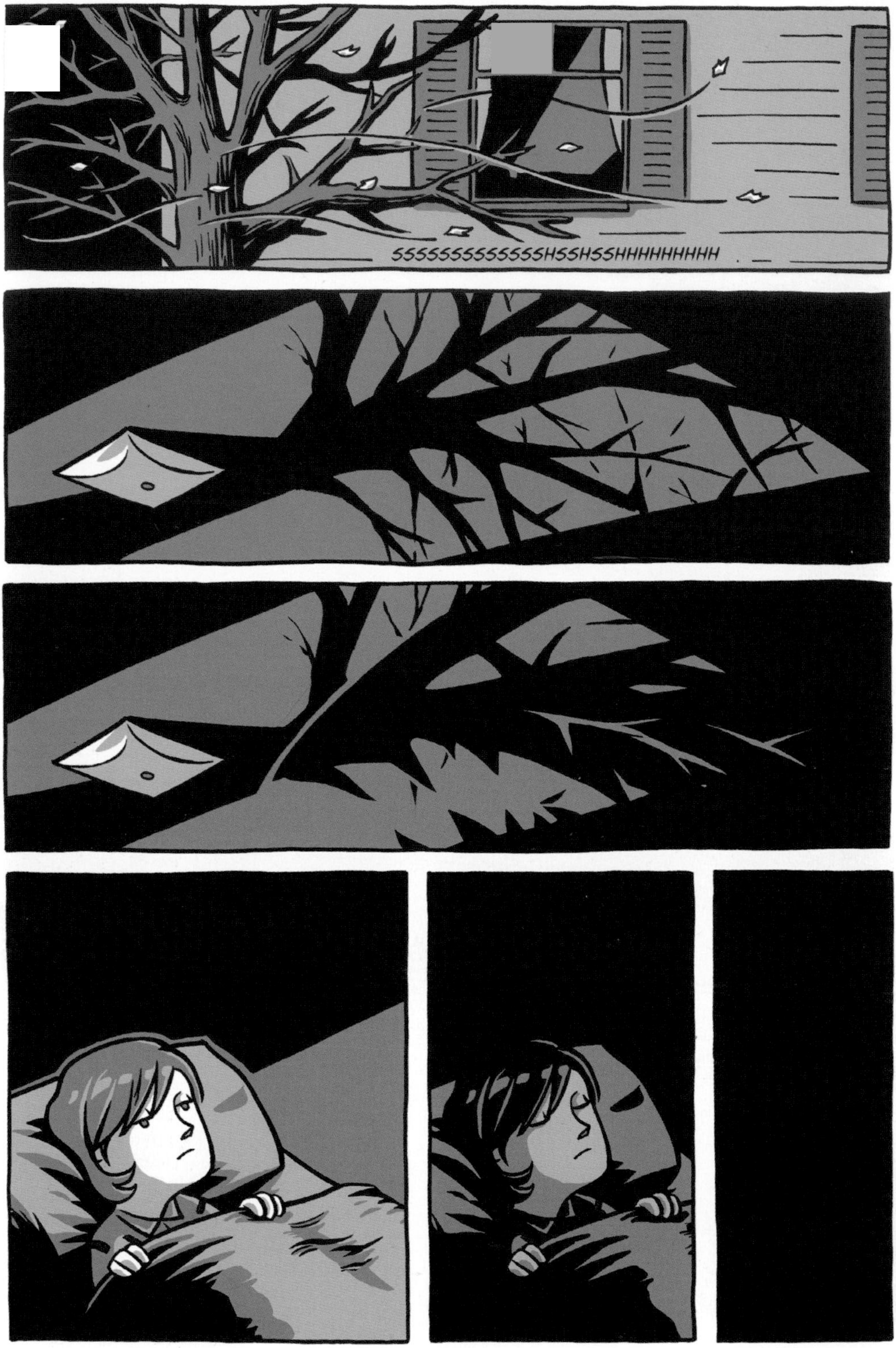
SSSSSSSSSSSSSHSSHSSHHHHHHHHH

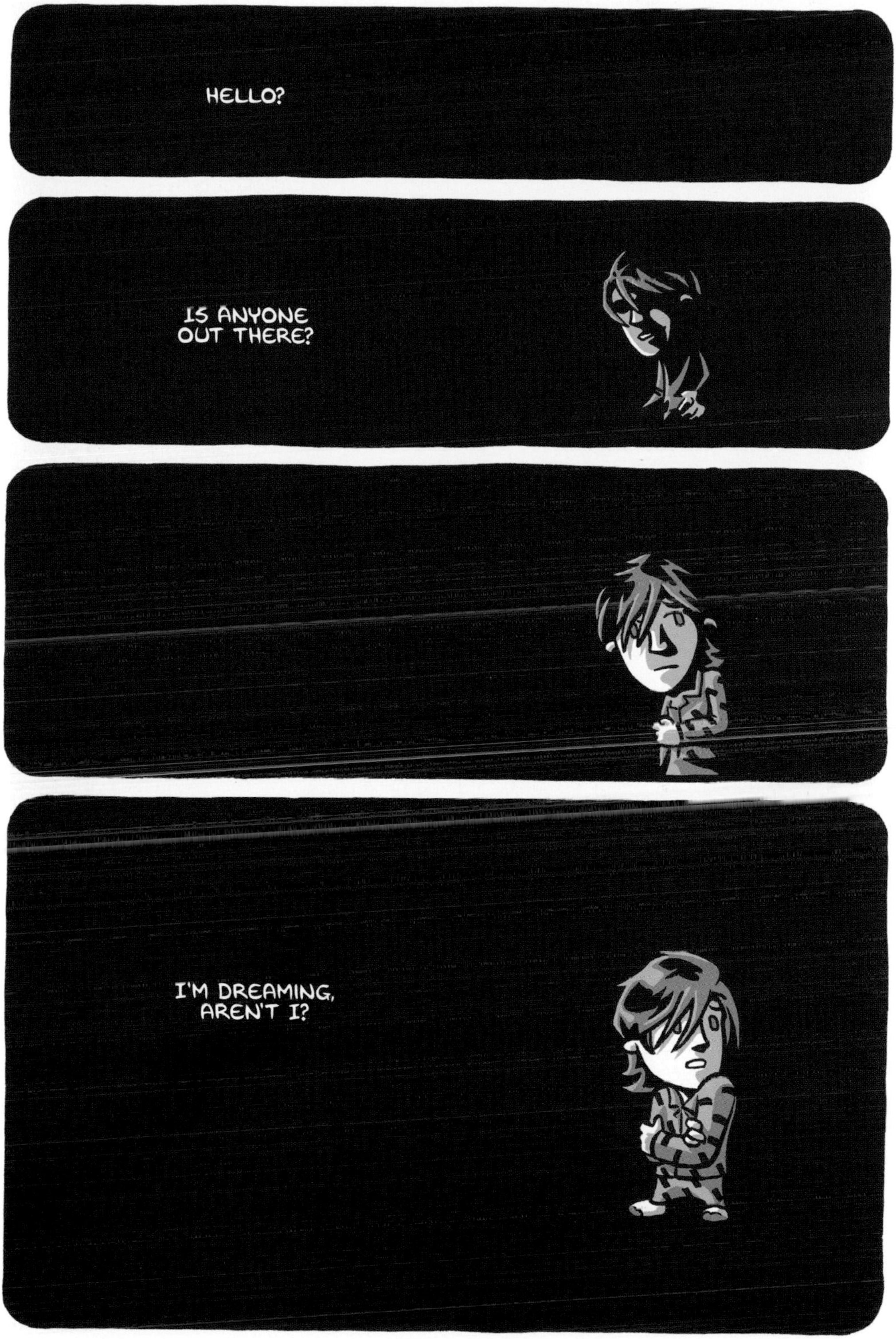
HELLO?
IS ANYONE OUT THERE?
I'M DREAMING, AREN'T I?

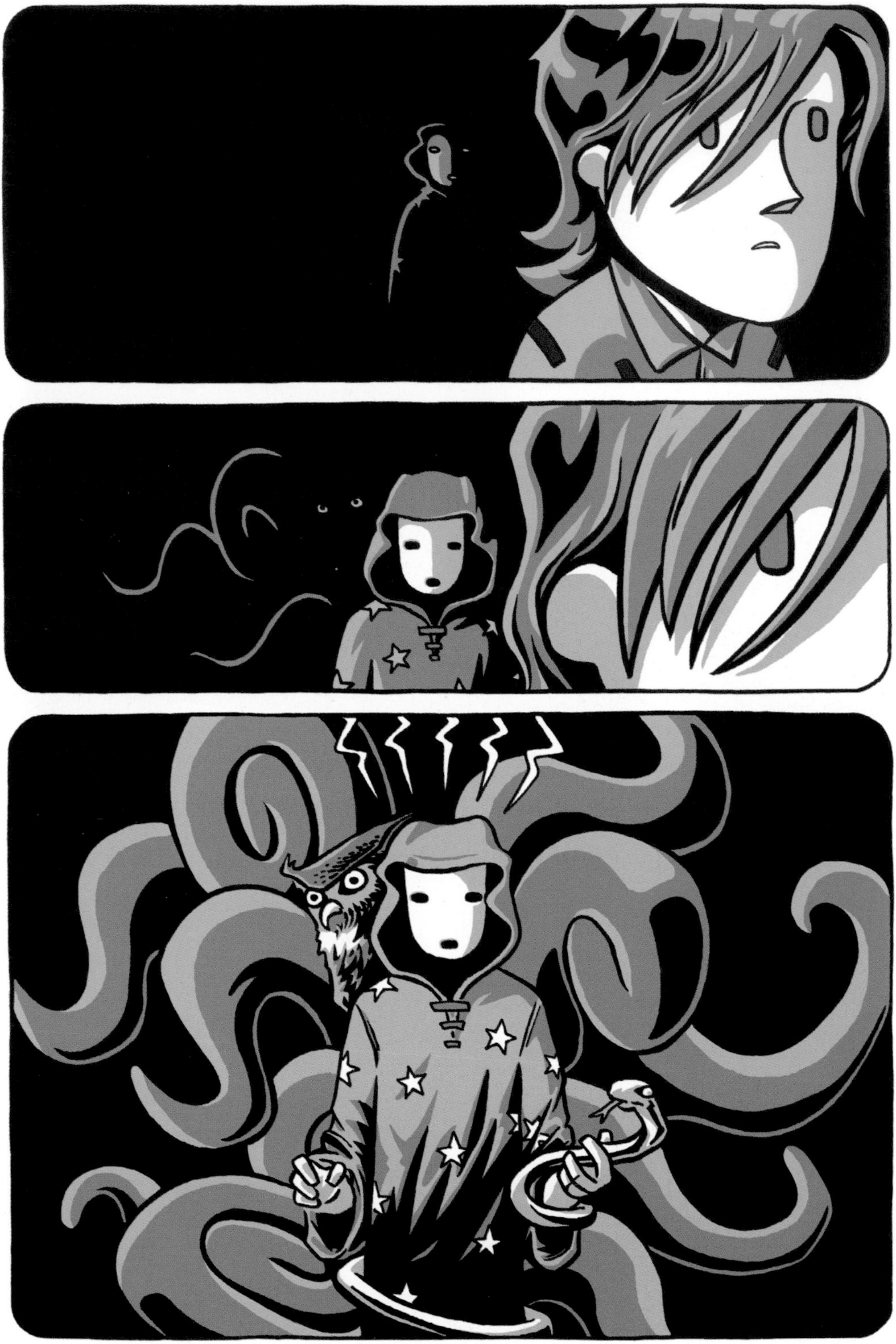

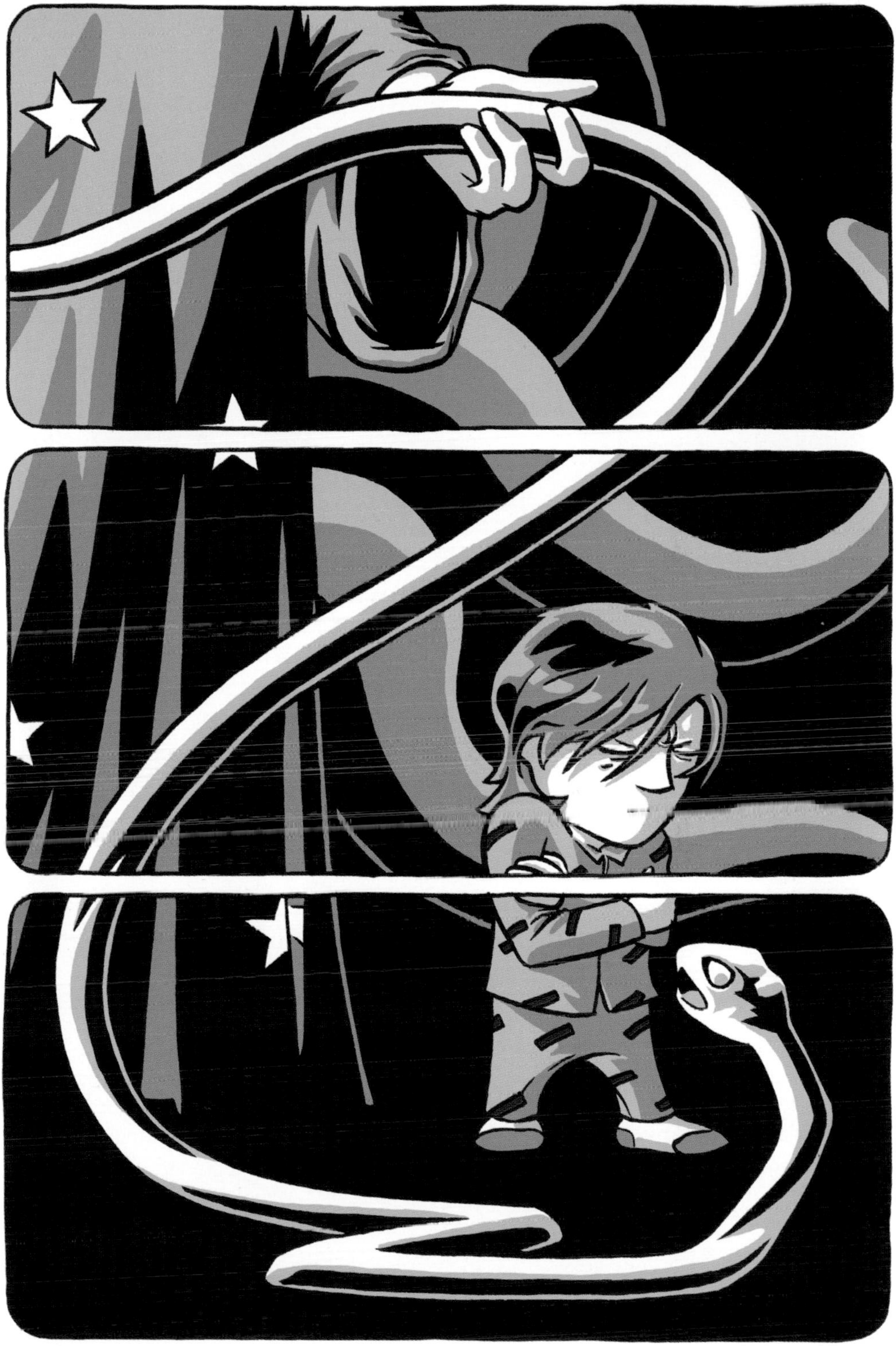

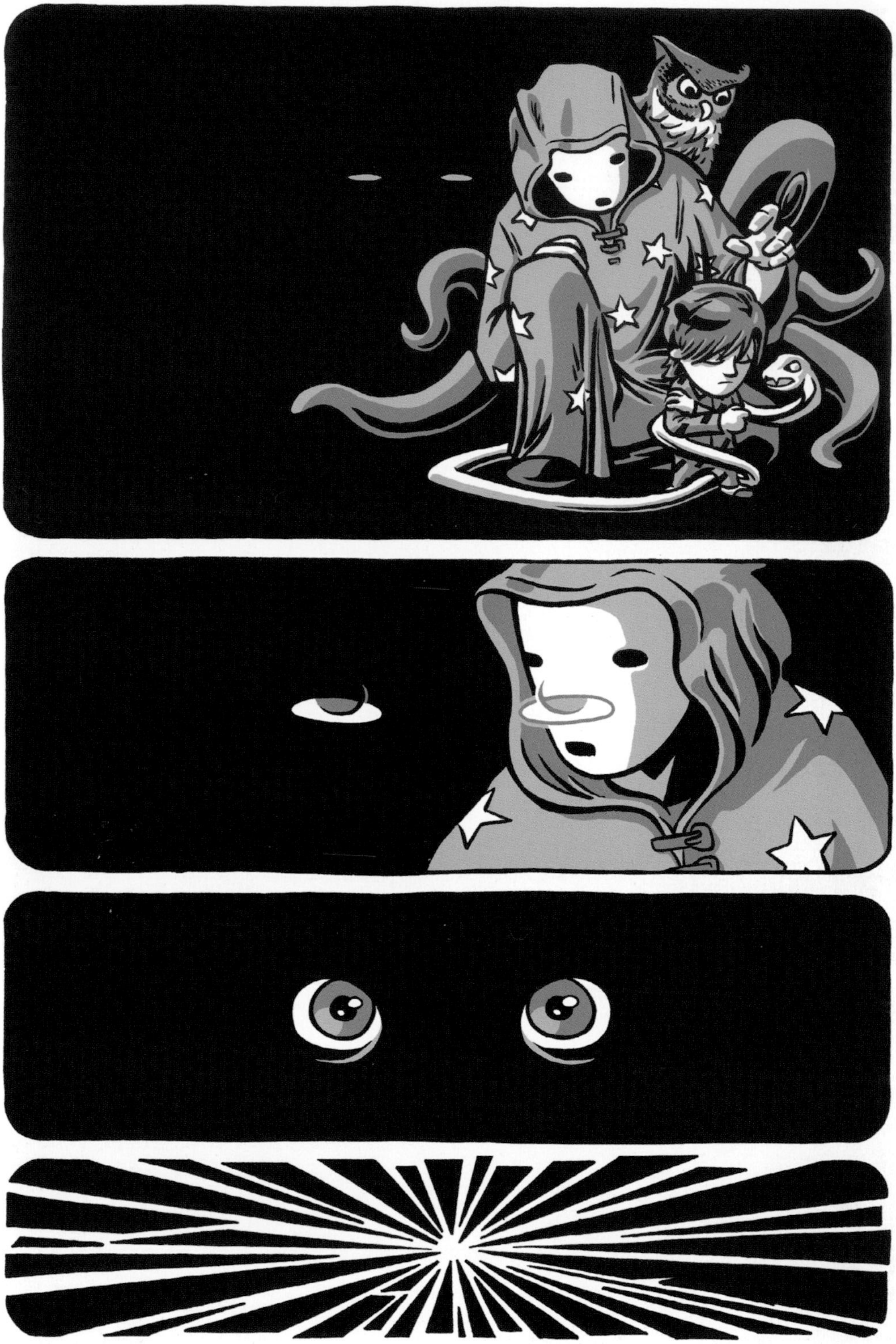

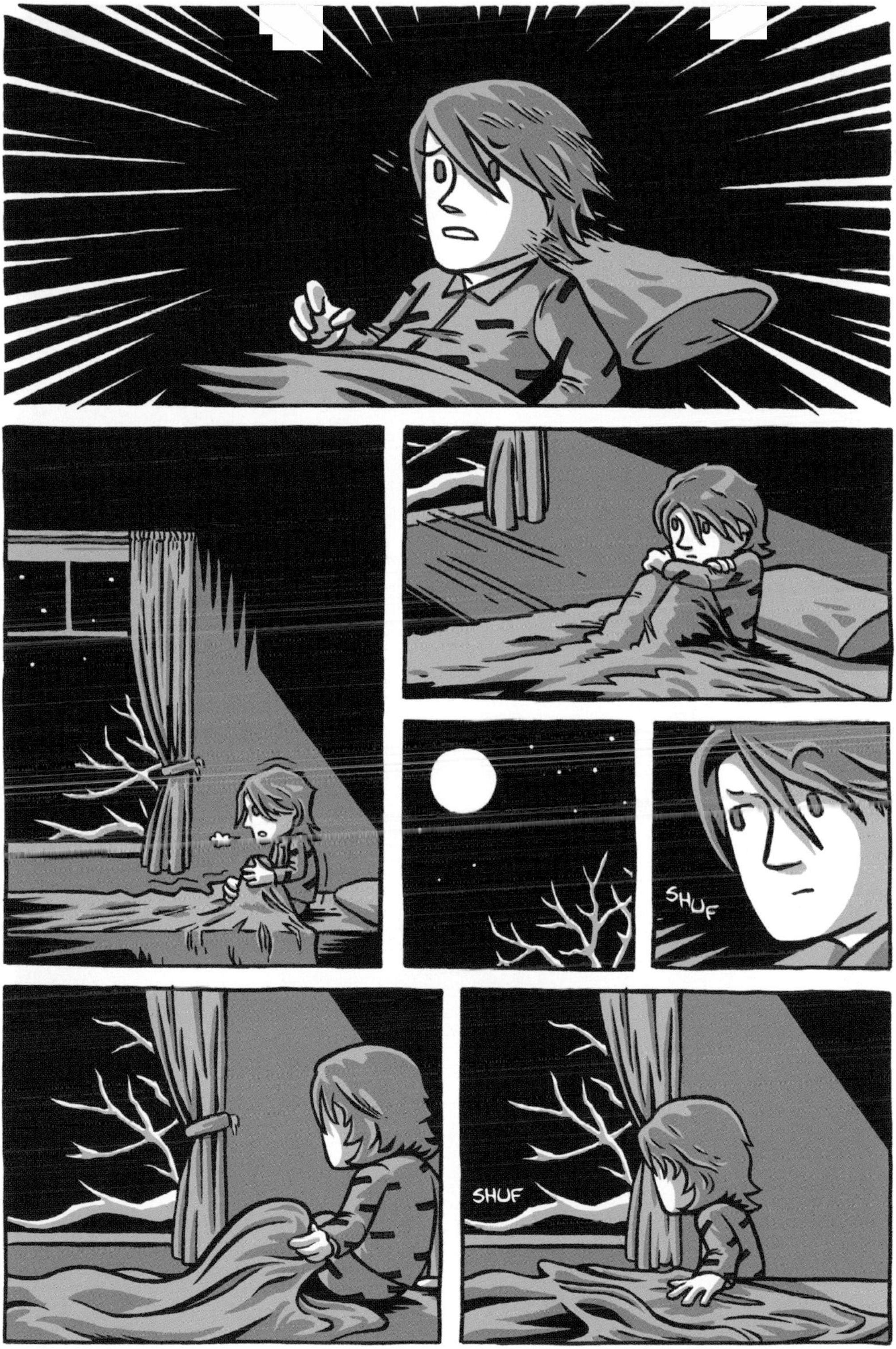
SHUF
SHUF

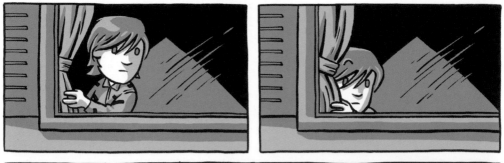

SHUF

24

CREEEEEE...

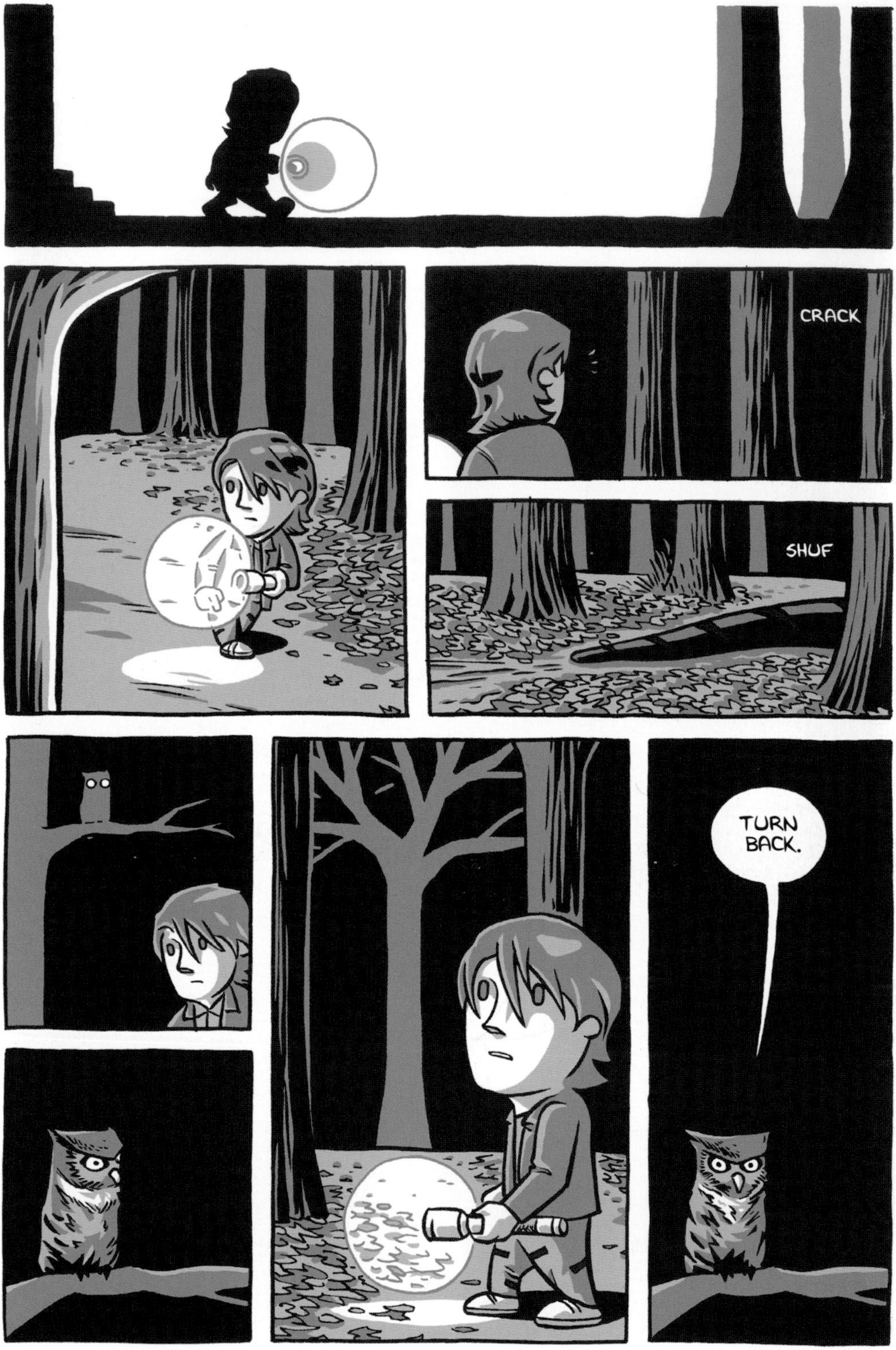
CRACK
SHUF
TURN BACK.

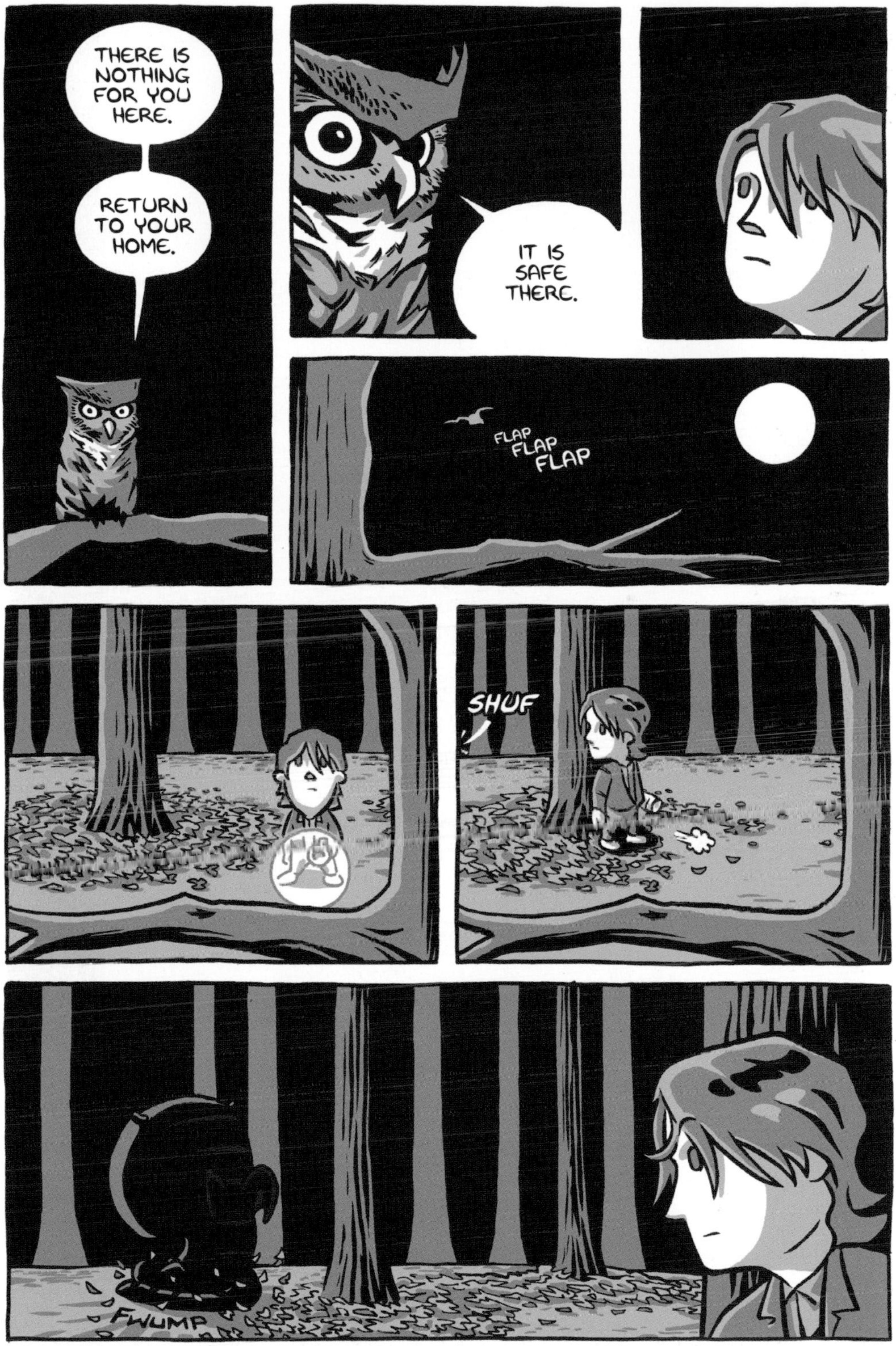
THERE IS NOTHING FOR YOU HERE.
RETURN TO YOUR HOME.
IT IS SAFE THERE.
FLAP FLAP FLAP
SHUF
FWUMP

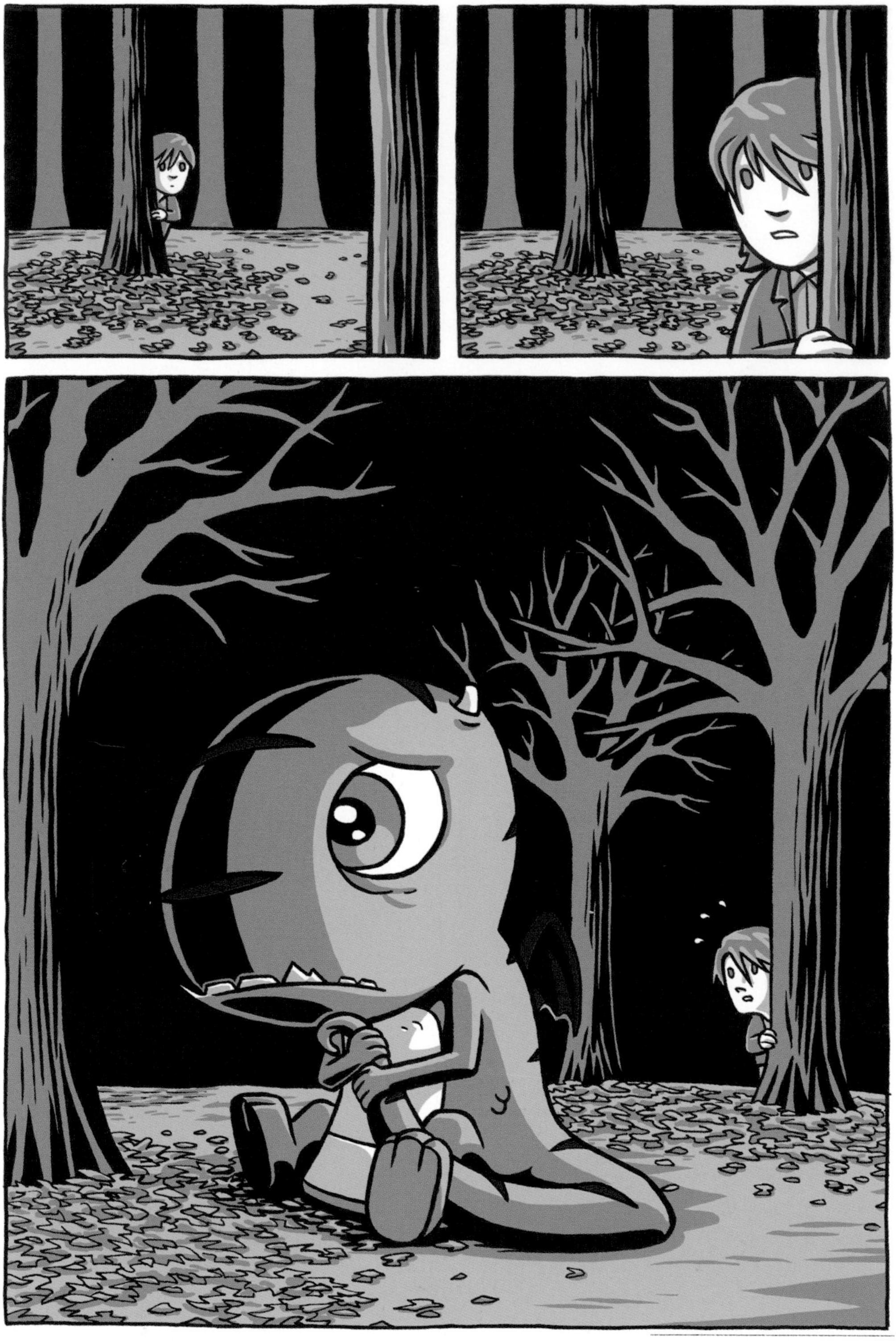

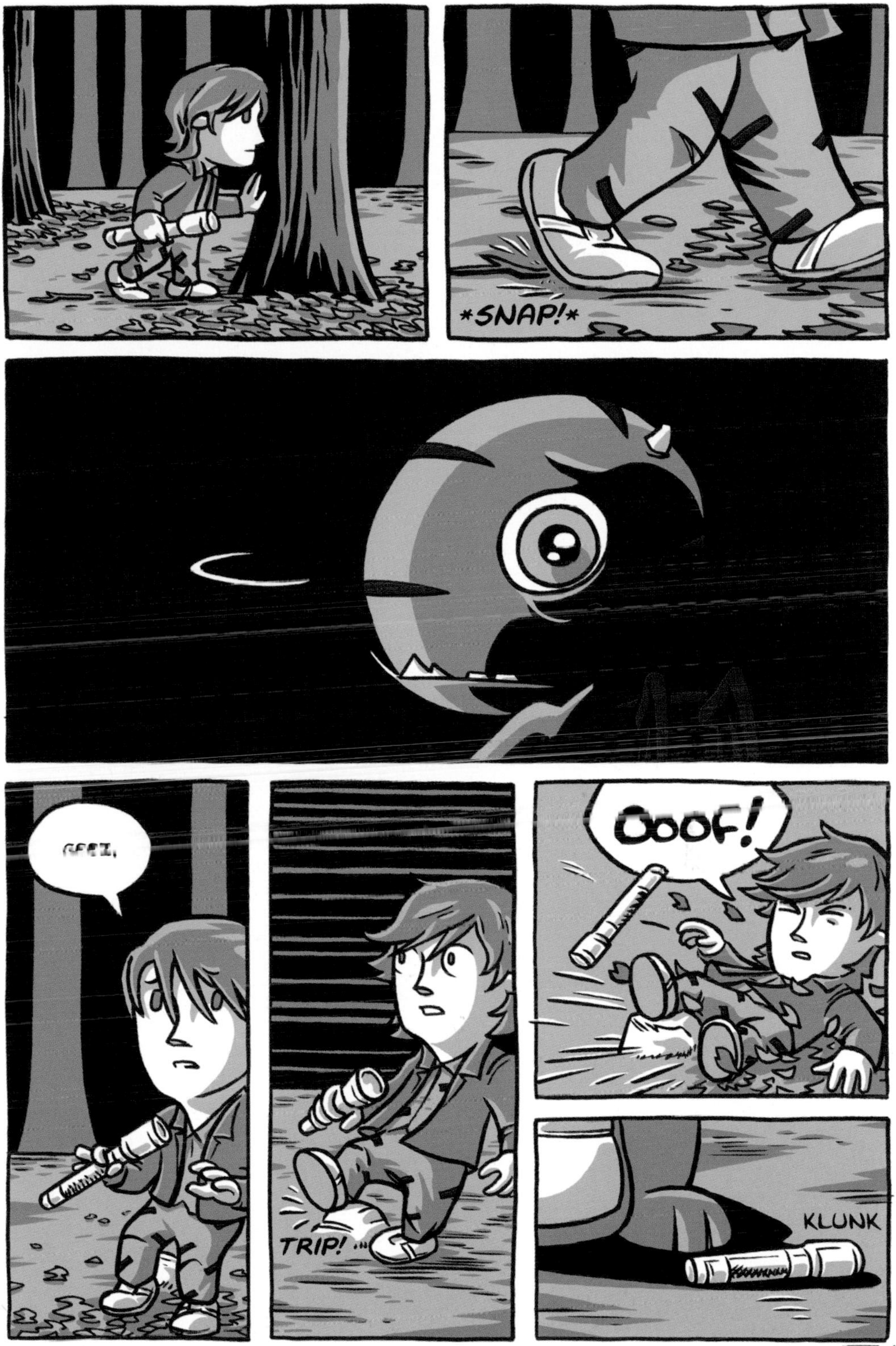
SNAP!
OOOF!
TRIP!
KLUNK

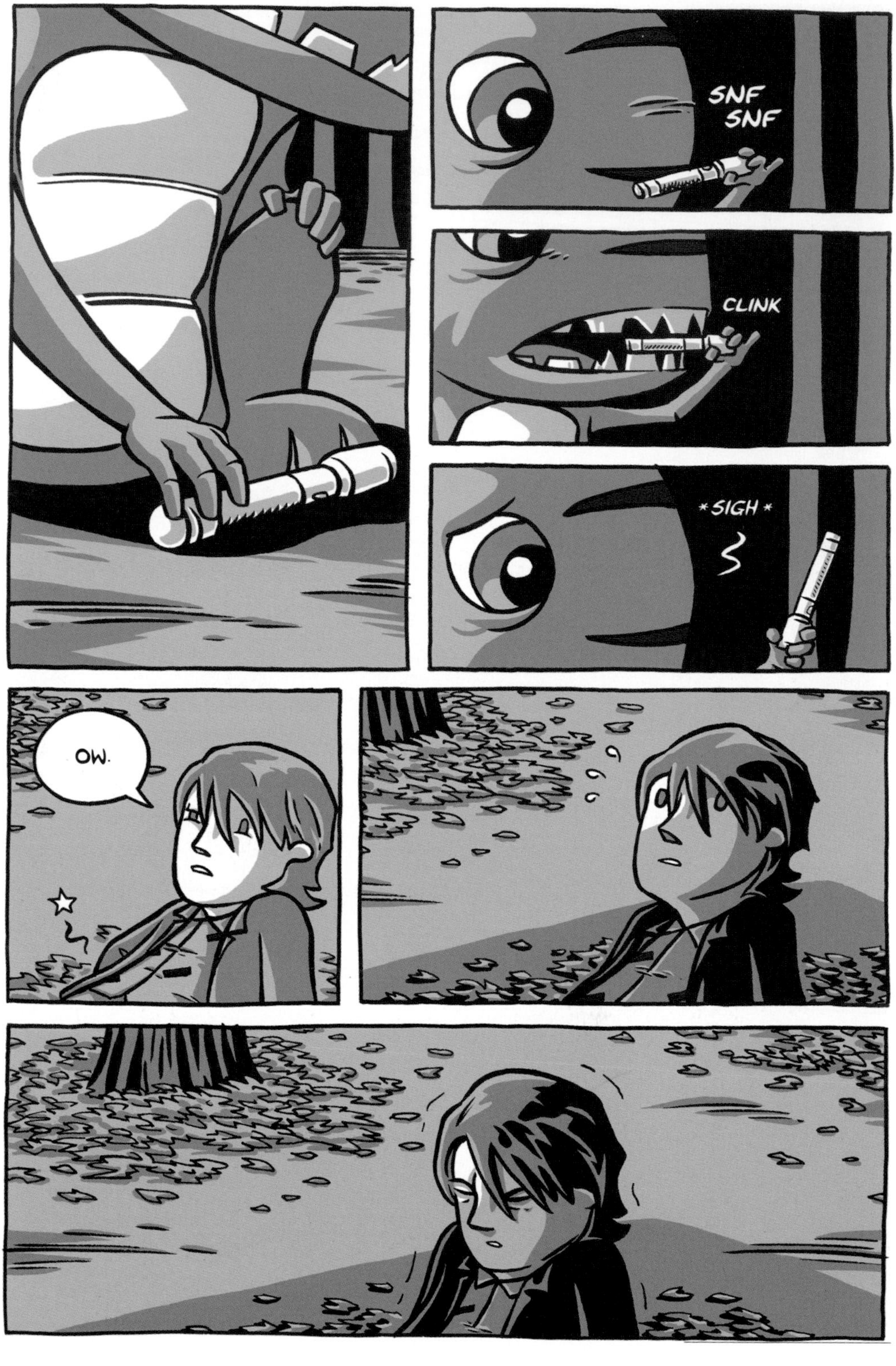
SNF
SNF
CLINK
SIGH
OW.

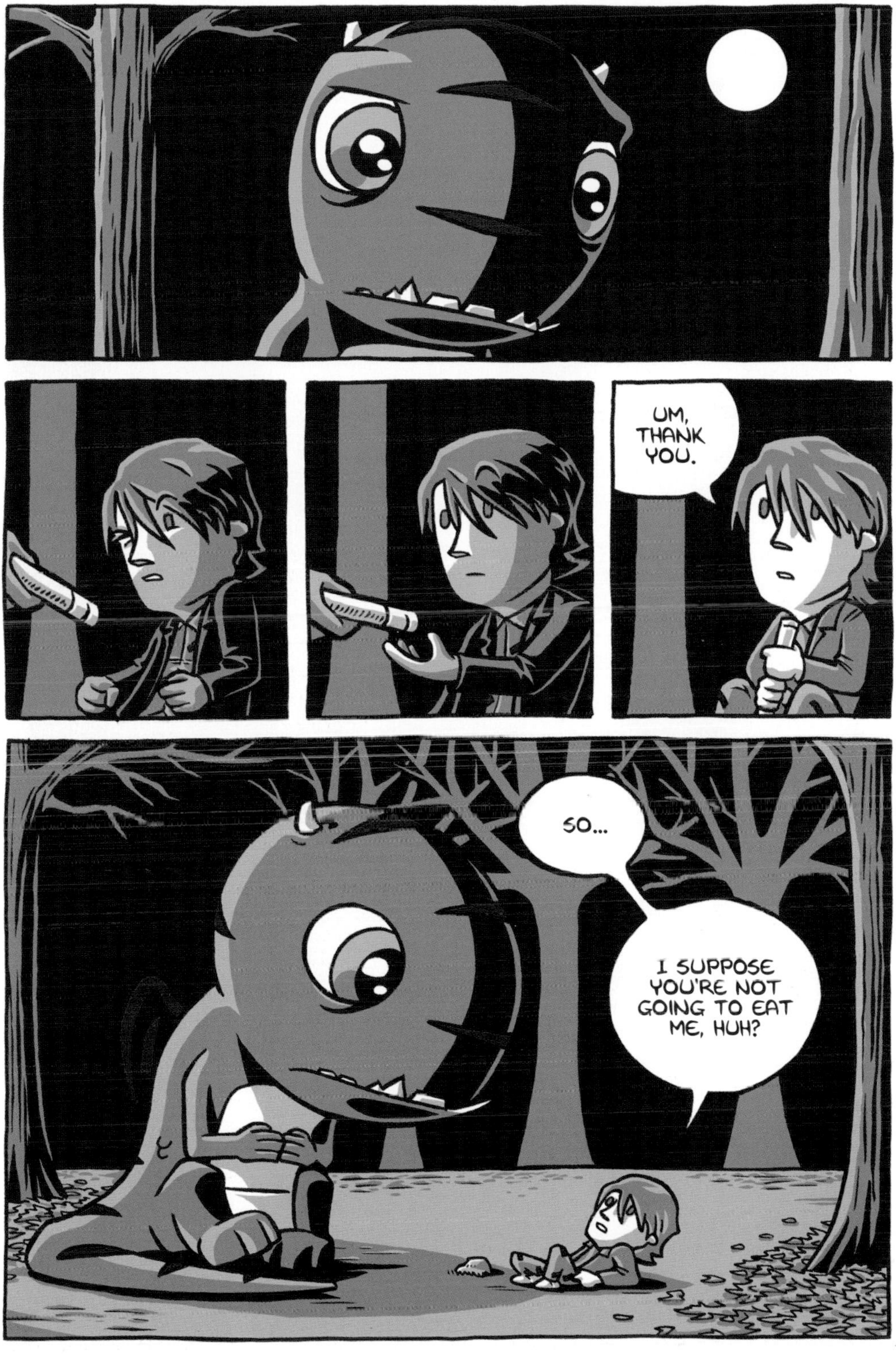
UM, THANK YOU.
SO...
I SUPPOSE YOU'RE NOT GOING TO EAT ME, HUH?

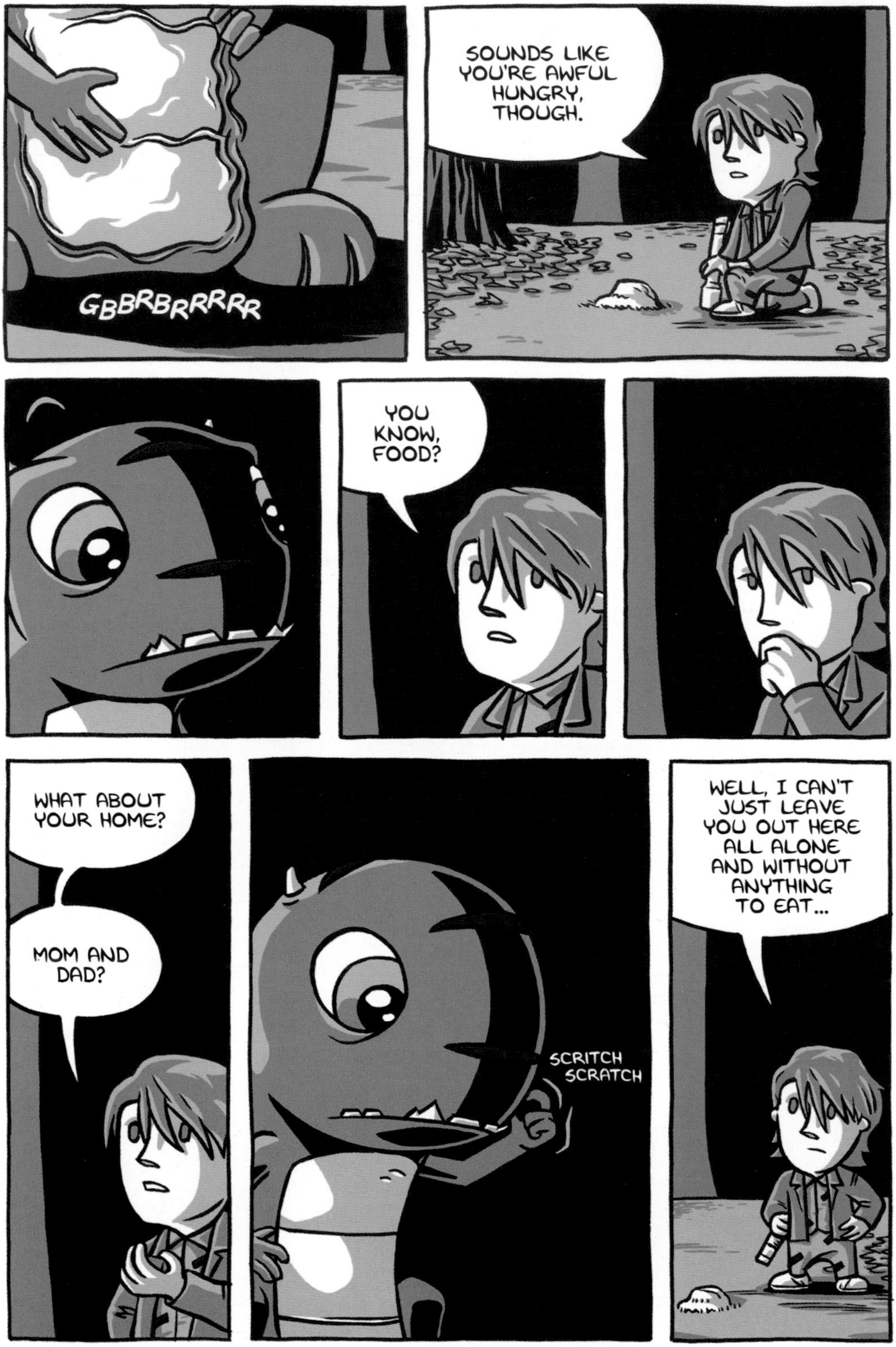
GBBRBRRRRR
SOUNDS LIKE YOU'RE AWFUL HUNGRY, THOUGH.
YOU KNOW, FOOD?
WHAT ABOUT YOUR HOME?
MOM AND DAD?
SCRITCH SCRATCH
WELL, I CAN'T JUST LEAVE YOU OUT HERE ALL ALONE AND WITHOUT ANYTHING TO EAT...

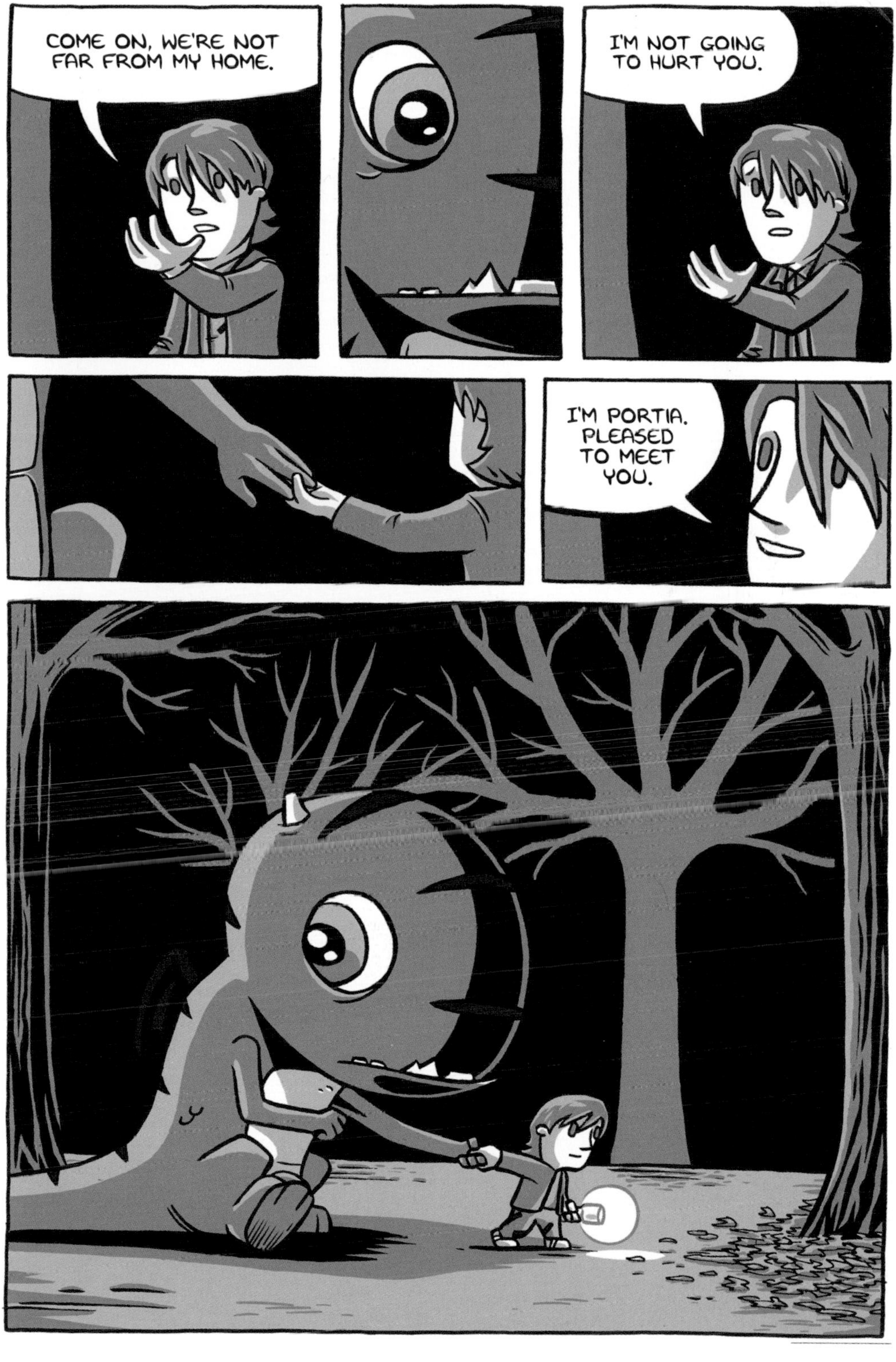
COME ON, WE'RE NOT FAR FROM MY HOME.
I'M NOT GOING TO HURT YOU.
I'M PORTIA. PLEASED TO MEET YOU.

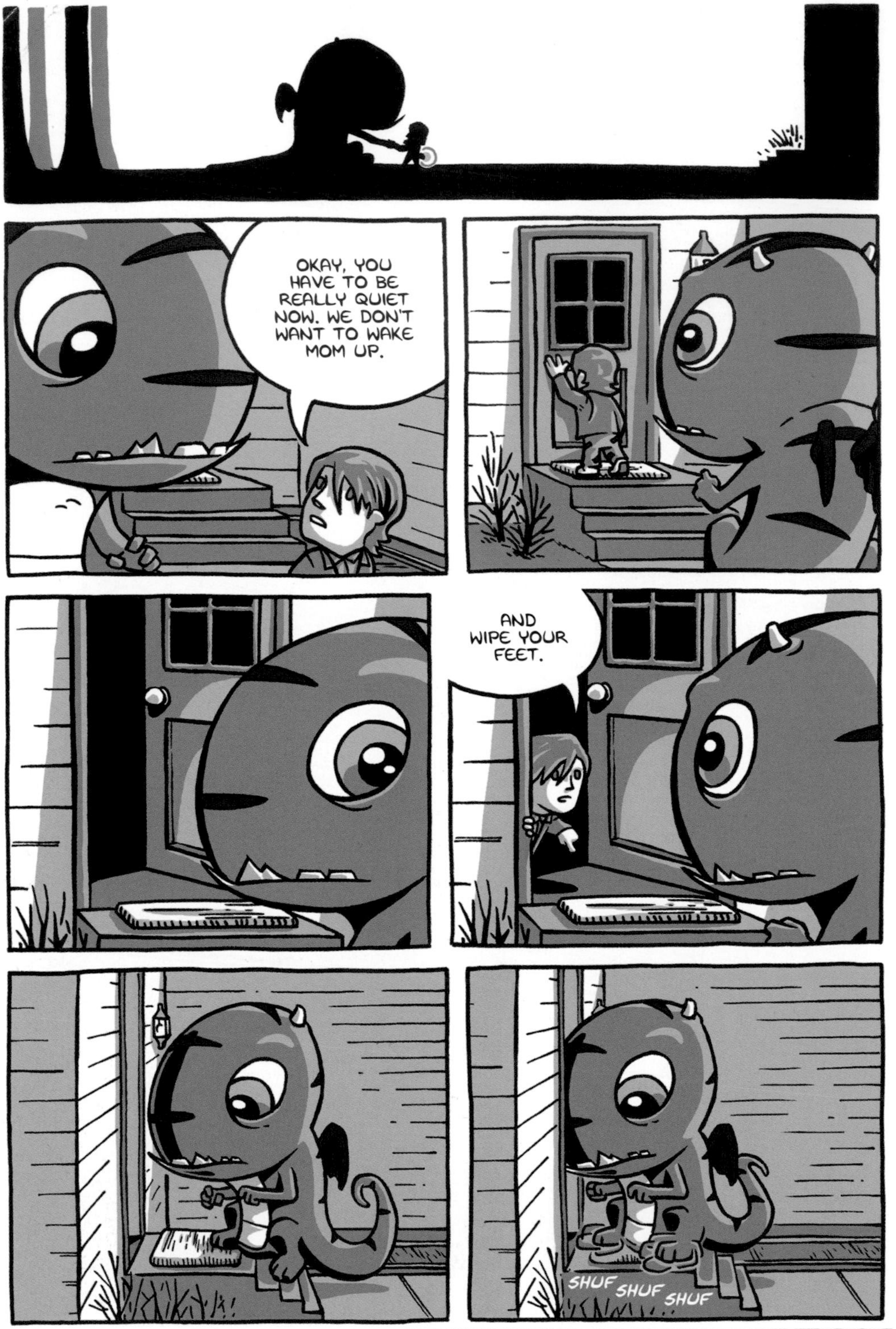
OKAY, YOU HAVE TO BE REALLY QUIET NOW. WE DON'T WANT TO WAKE MOM UP.
AND WIPE YOUR FEET.
SHUF SHUF SHUF

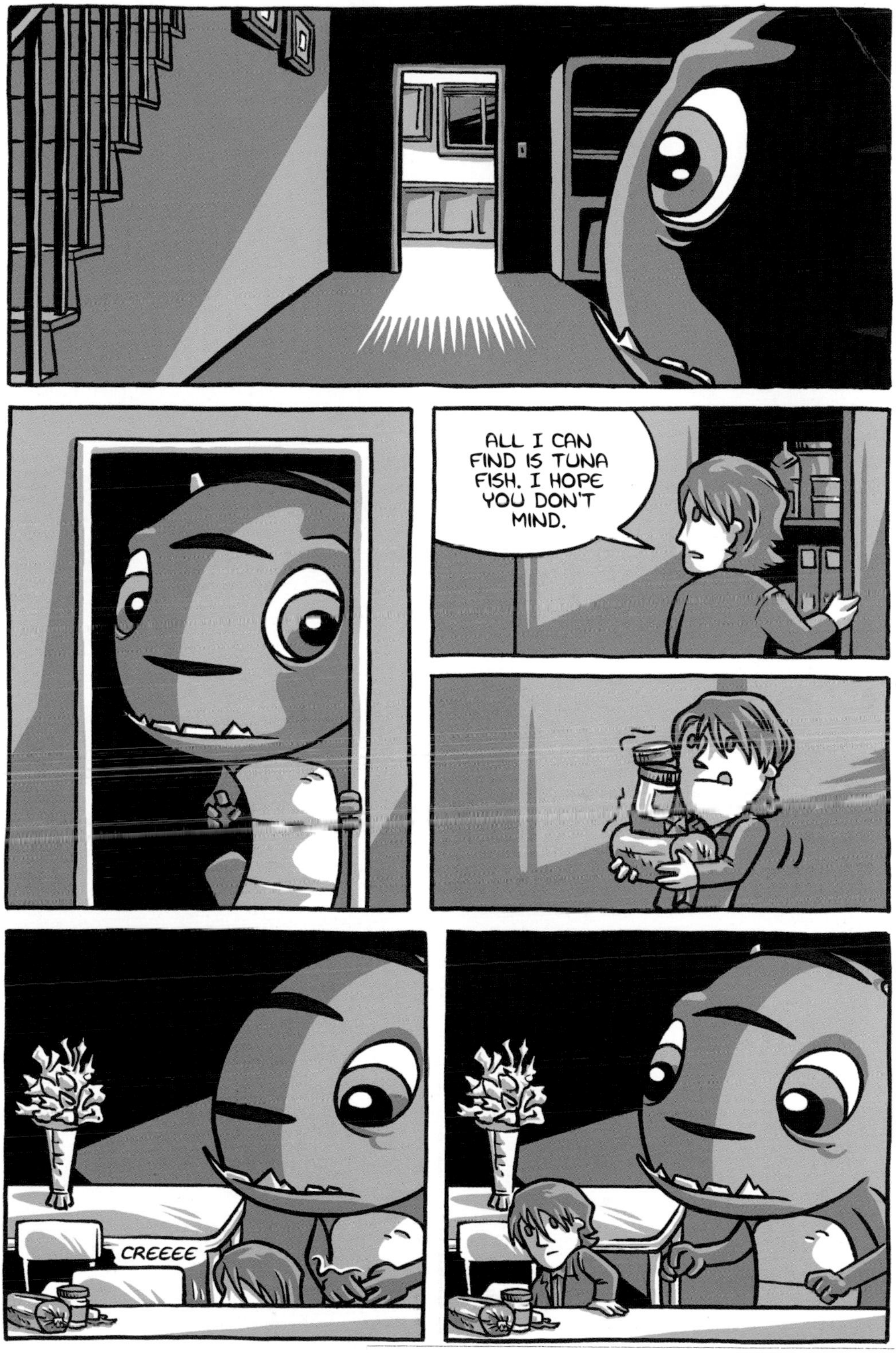
ALL I CAN FIND IS TUNA FISH. I HOPE YOU DON'T MIND.
CREEEE

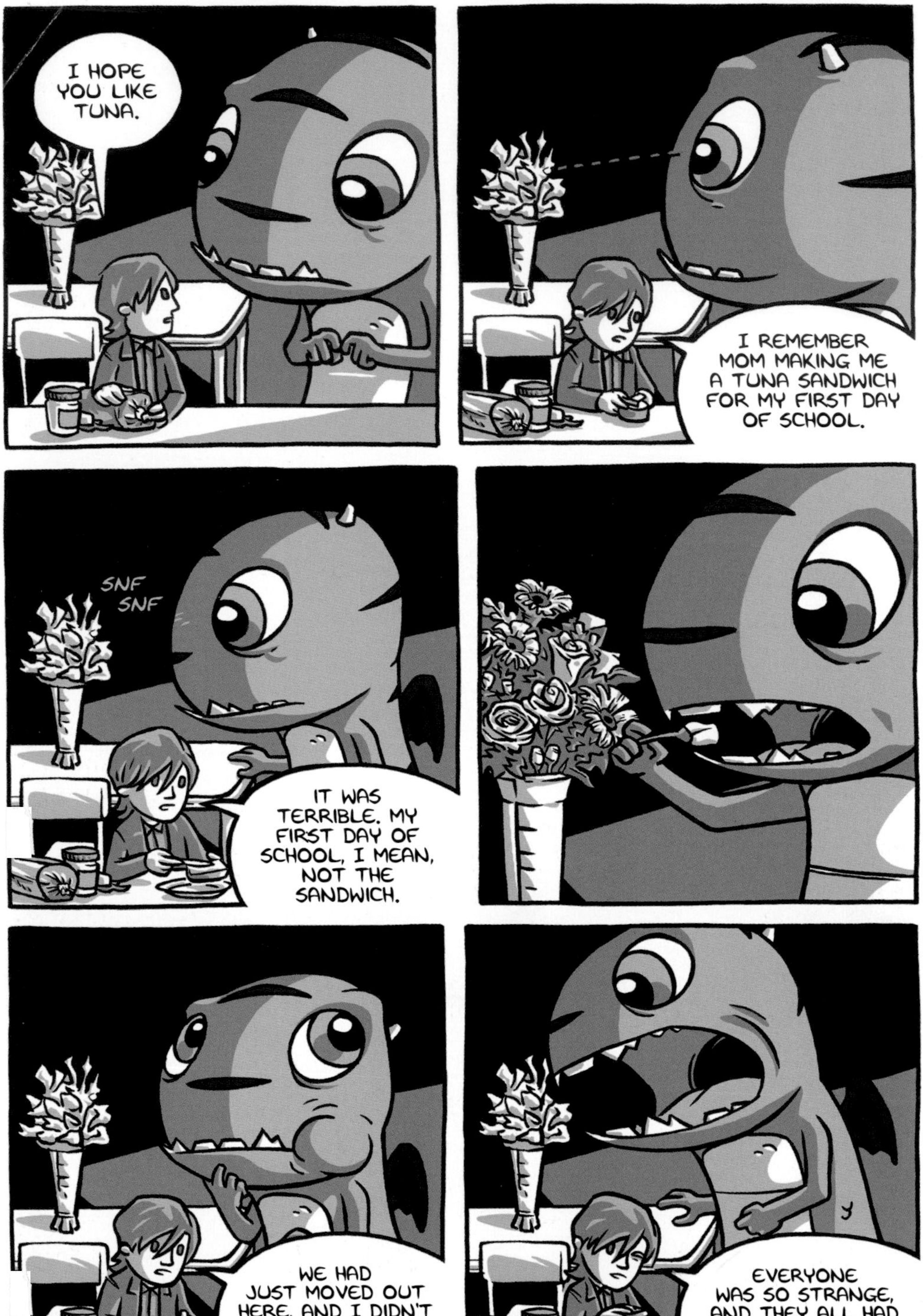
I HOPE YOU LIKE TUNA.
I REMEMBER MOM MAKING ME A TUNA SANDWICH FOR MY FIRST DAY OF SCHOOL.
SNF SNF
IT WAS TERRIBLE. MY FIRST DAY OF SCHOOL, I MEAN, NOT THE SANDWICH.
WE HAD JUST MOVED OUT HERE, AND I DIDN'T KNOW ANYONE AT ALL.
EVERYONE WAS SO STRANGE, AND THEY ALL HAD THEIR OWN FRIENDS ANYWAY.

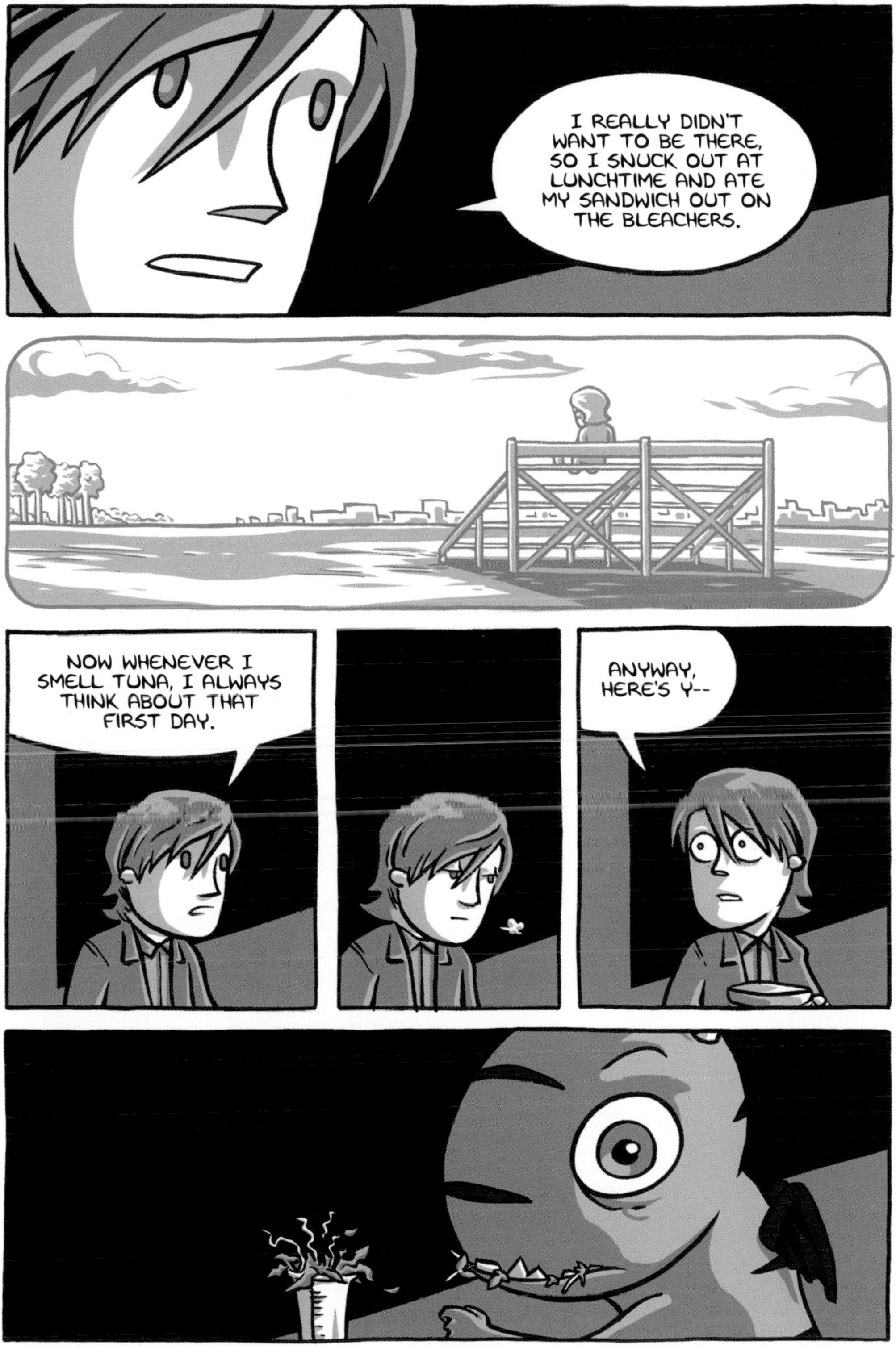
I REALLY DIDN'T WANT TO BE THERE, SO I SNUCK OUT AT LUNCHTIME AND ATE MY SANDWICH OUT ON THE BLEACHERS.
NOW WHENEVER I SMELL TUNA, I ALWAYS THINK ABOUT THAT FIRST DAY.
ANYWAY, HERE'S Y--

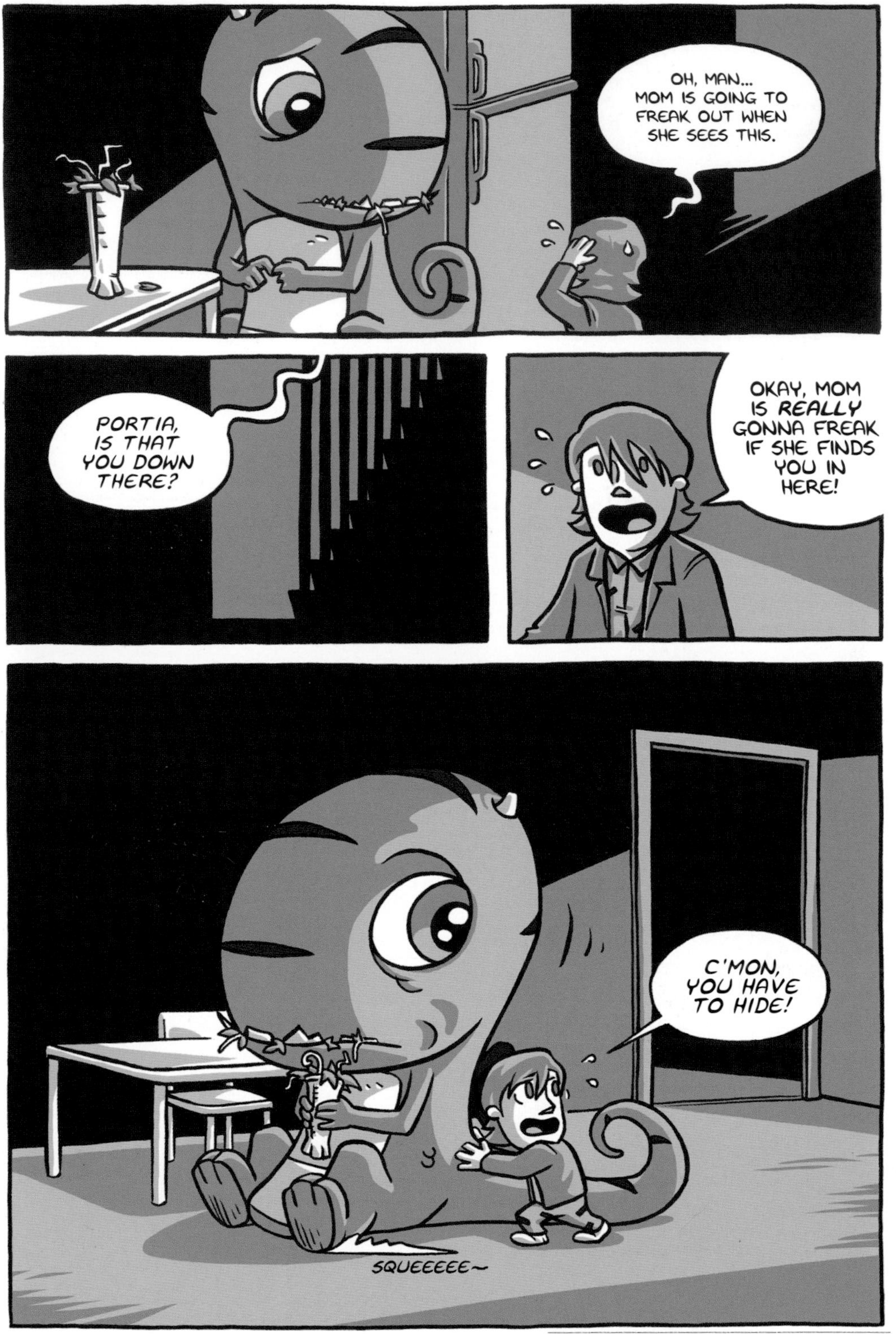

OH, MAN... MOM IS GOING TO FREAK OUT WHEN SHE SEES THIS.
PORTIA, IS THAT YOU DOWN THERE?
OKAY, MOM IS *REALLY* GONNA FREAK IF SHE FINDS YOU IN HERE!
C'MON, YOU HAVE TO HIDE!
SQUEEEEEE~

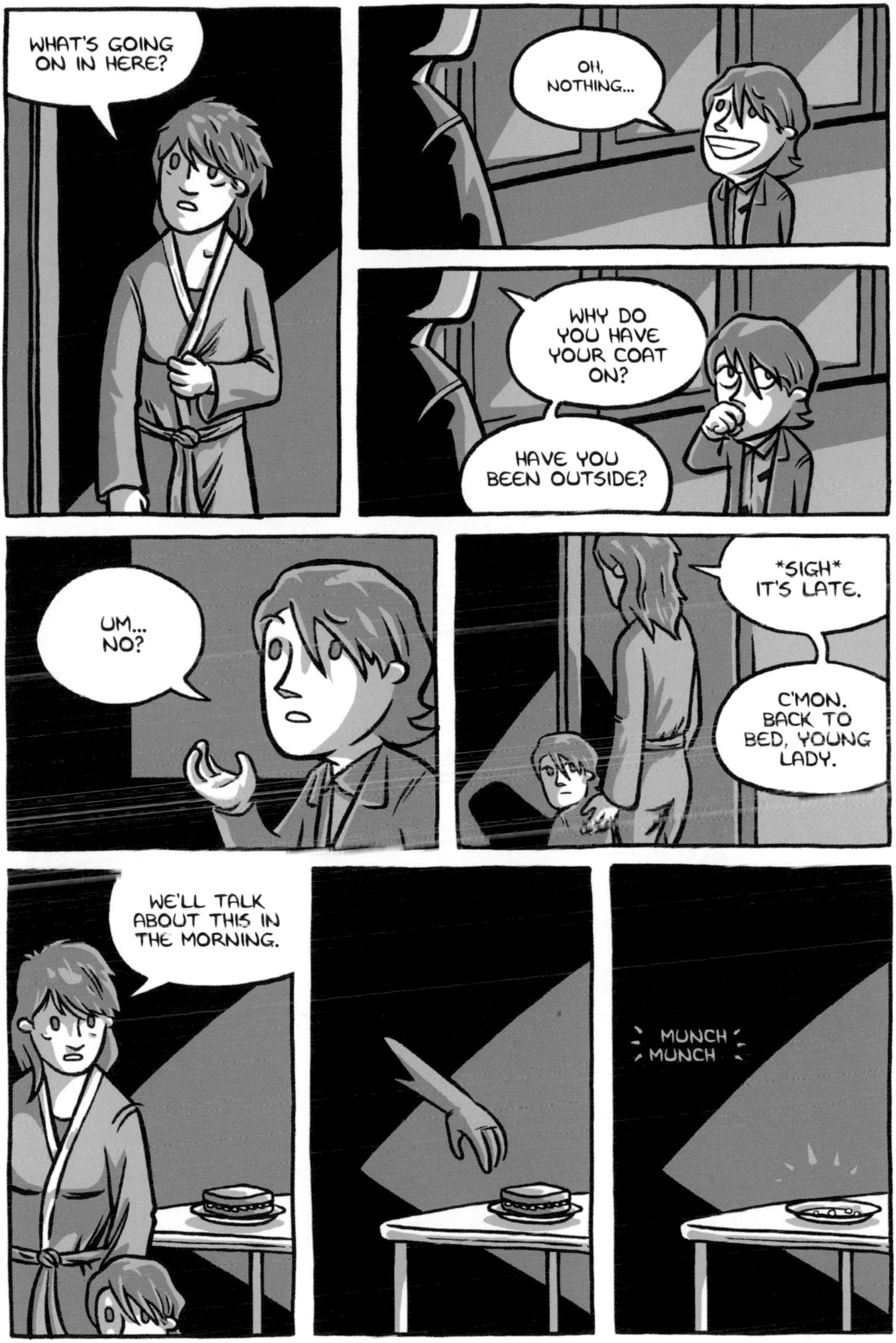
WHAT'S GOING ON IN HERE?
OH, NOTHING...
WHY DO YOU HAVE YOUR COAT ON?
HAVE YOU BEEN OUTSIDE?
UM... NO?
SIGH IT'S LATE.
C'MON. BACK TO BED, YOUNG LADY.
WE'LL TALK ABOUT THIS IN THE MORNING.
MUNCH MUNCH

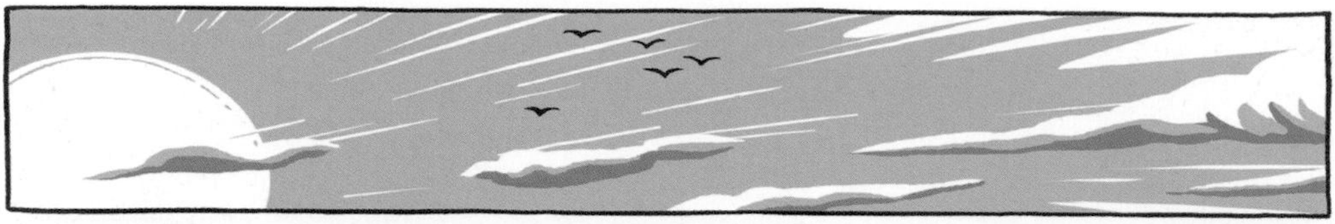

CHAPTER TWO

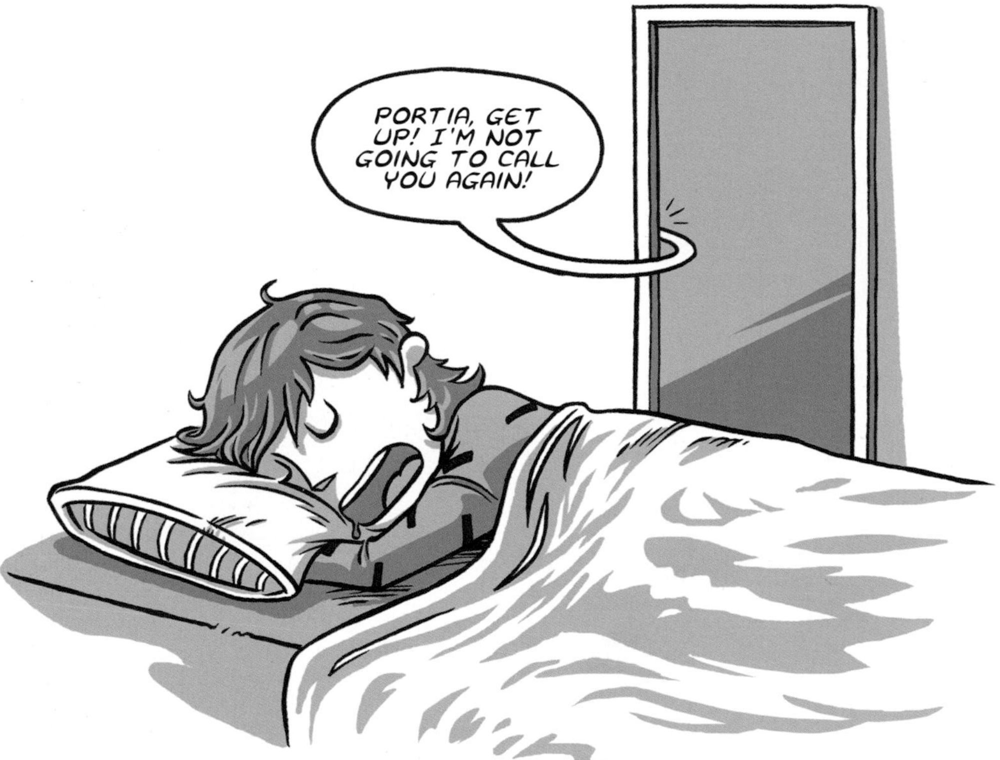
PORTIA, GET UP! I'M NOT GOING TO CALL YOU AGAIN!

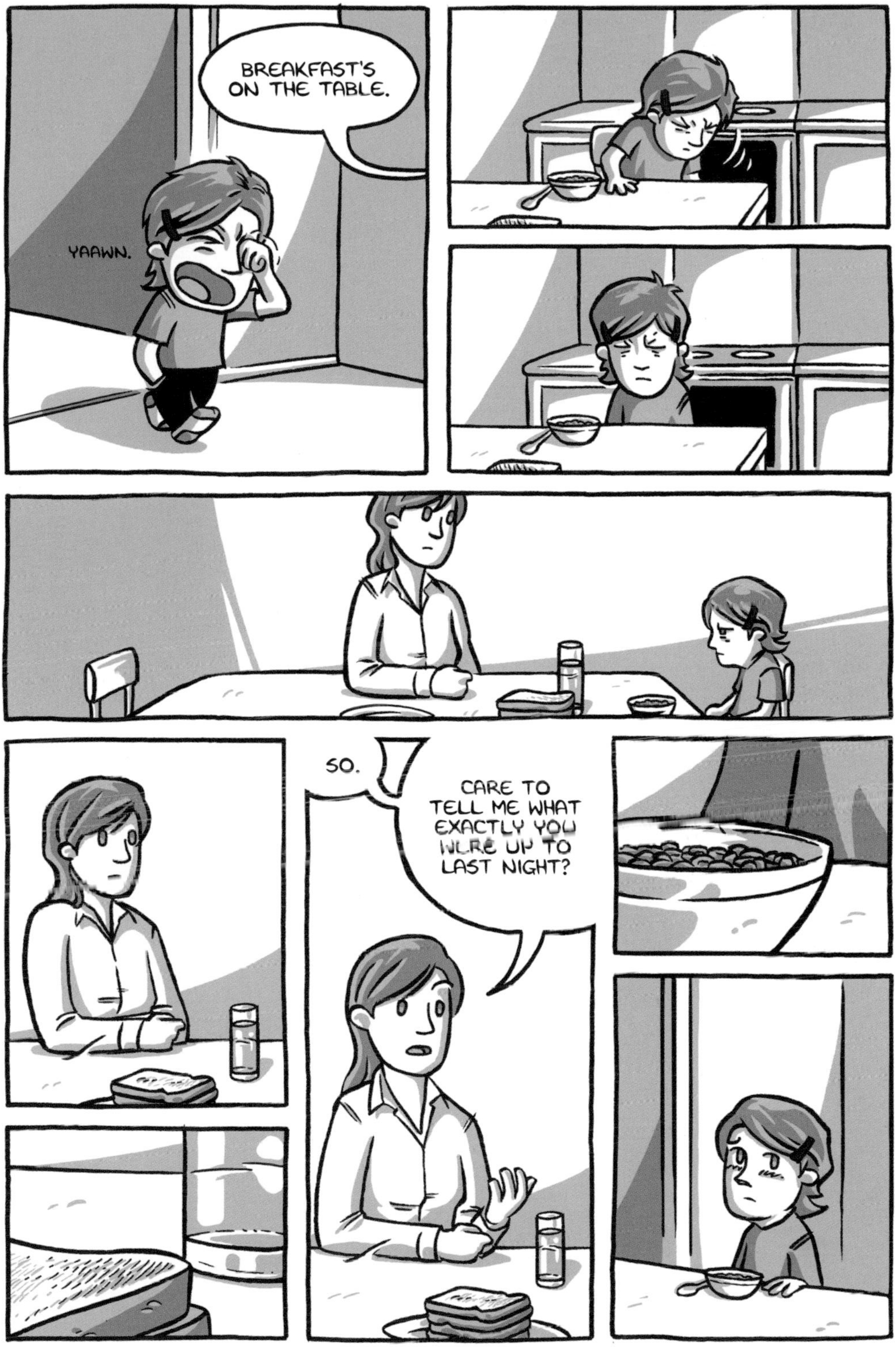
BREAKFAST'S ON THE TABLE.
YAAWN.
SO.
CARE TO TELL ME WHAT EXACTLY YOU WERE UP TO LAST NIGHT?

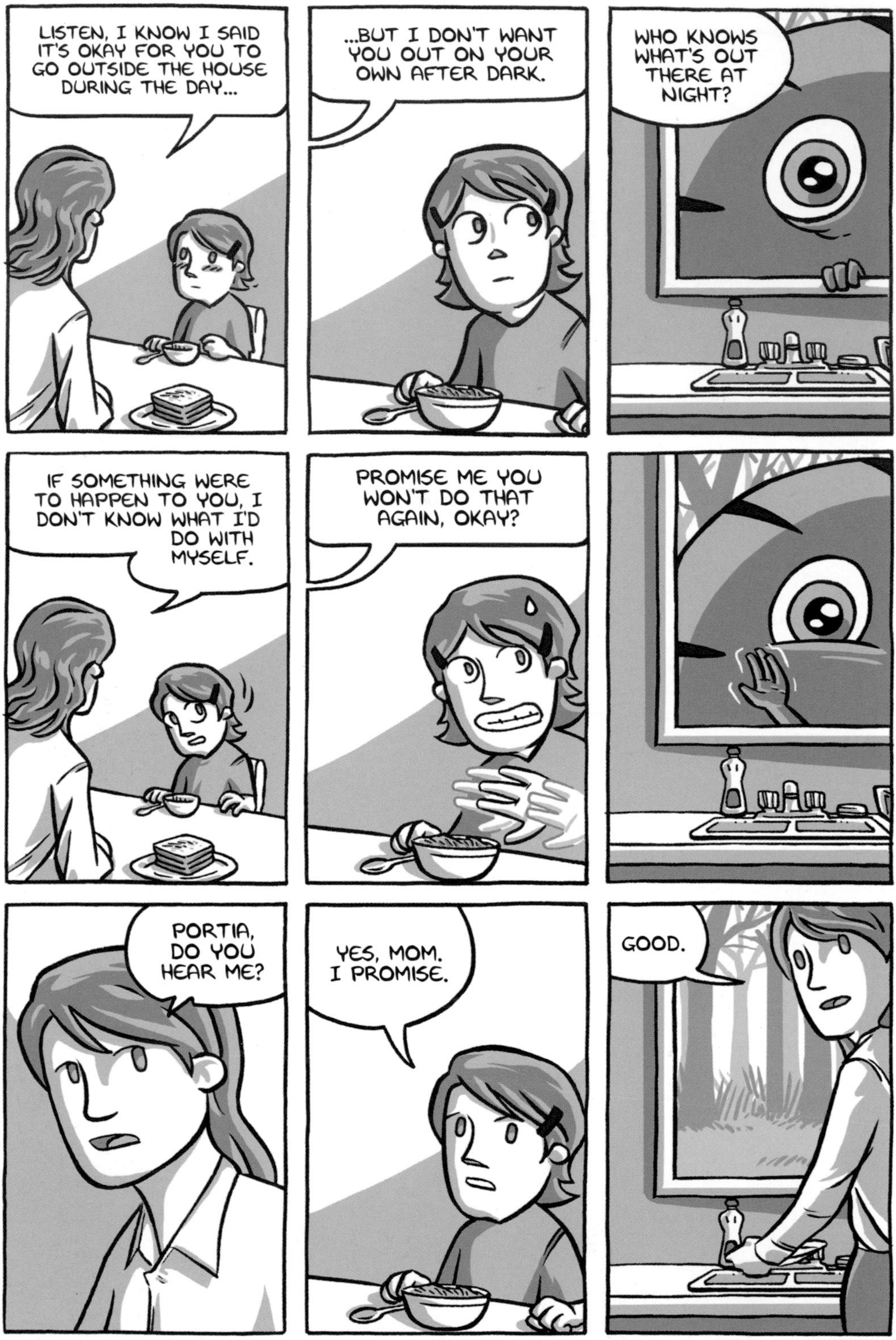
LISTEN, I KNOW I SAID IT'S OKAY FOR YOU TO GO OUTSIDE THE HOUSE DURING THE DAY...
...BUT I DON'T WANT YOU OUT ON YOUR OWN AFTER DARK.
WHO KNOWS WHAT'S OUT THERE AT NIGHT?
IF SOMETHING WERE TO HAPPEN TO YOU, I DON'T KNOW WHAT I'D DO WITH MYSELF.
PROMISE ME YOU WON'T DO THAT AGAIN, OKAY?
PORTIA, DO YOU HEAR ME?
YES, MOM. I PROMISE.
GOOD.

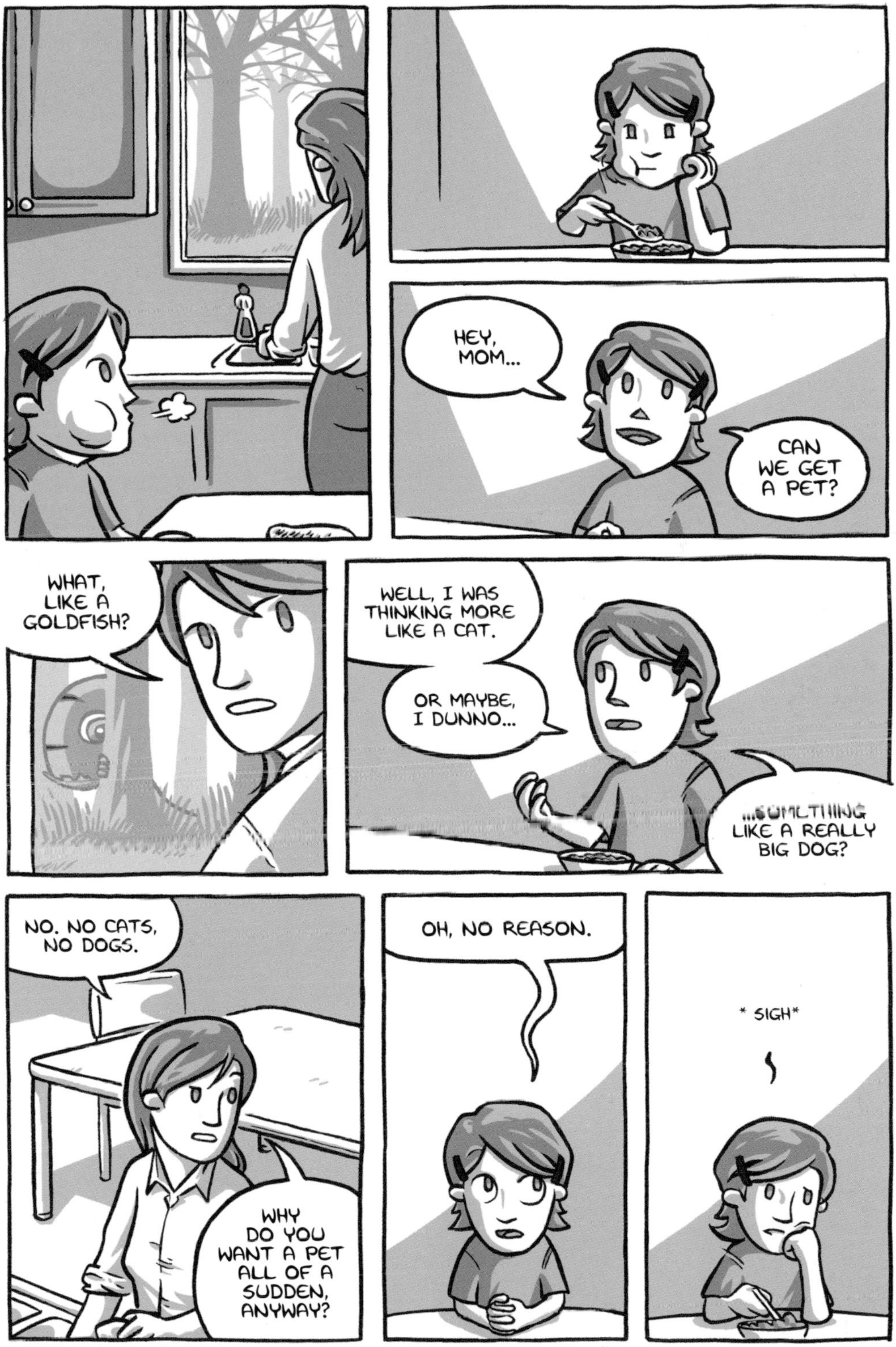

HEY, MOM...
CAN WE GET A PET?
WHAT, LIKE A GOLDFISH?
WELL, I WAS THINKING MORE LIKE A CAT.
OR MAYBE, I DUNNO...
...SOMETHING LIKE A REALLY BIG DOG?
NO. NO CATS, NO DOGS.
WHY DO YOU WANT A PET ALL OF A SUDDEN, ANYWAY?
OH, NO REASON.
* SIGH*

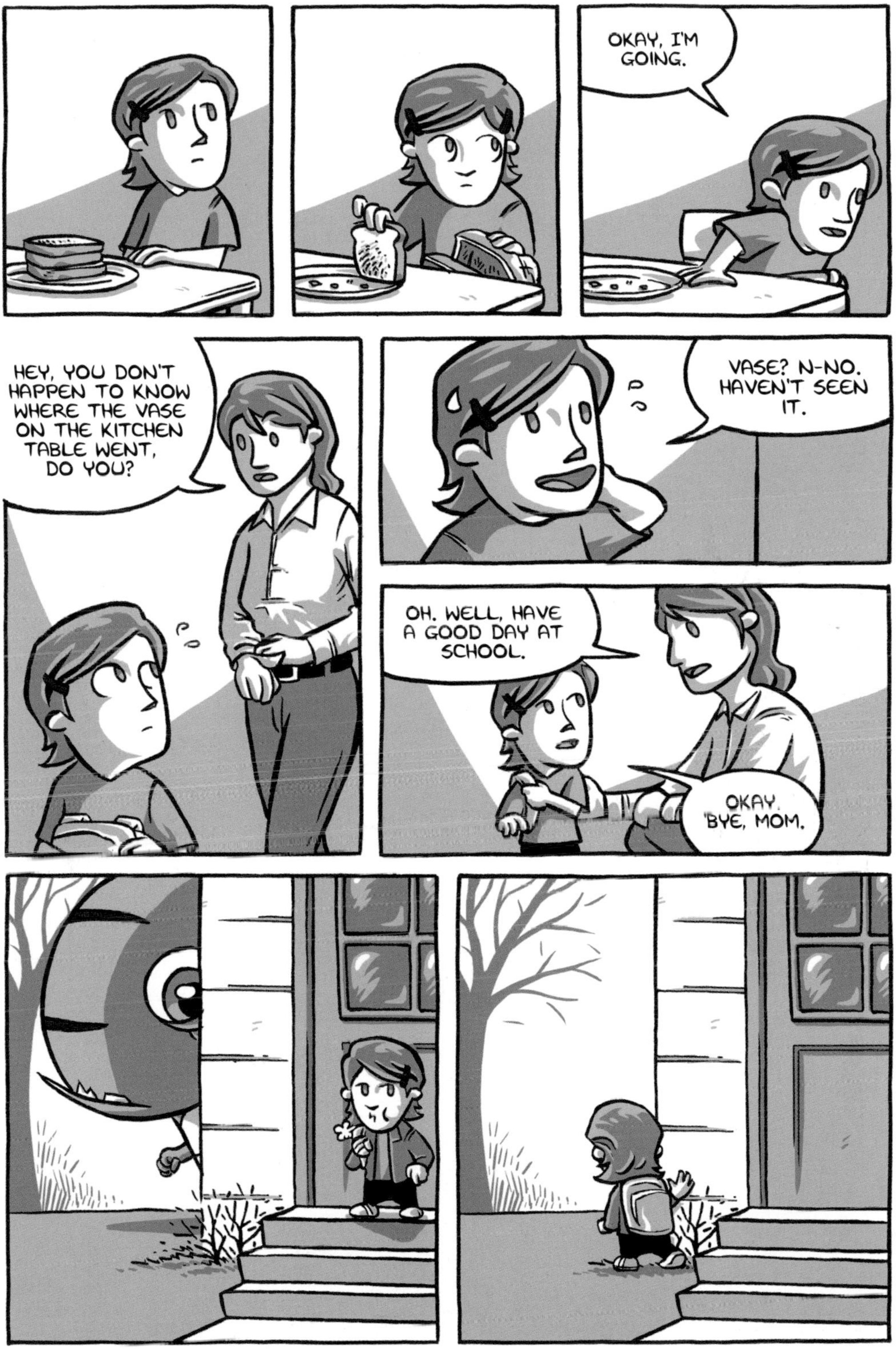
OKAY, I'M GOING.
HEY, YOU DON'T HAPPEN TO KNOW WHERE THE VASE ON THE KITCHEN TABLE WENT, DO YOU?
VASE? N-NO. HAVEN'T SEEN IT.
OH. WELL, HAVE A GOOD DAY AT SCHOOL.
OKAY. BYE, MOM.

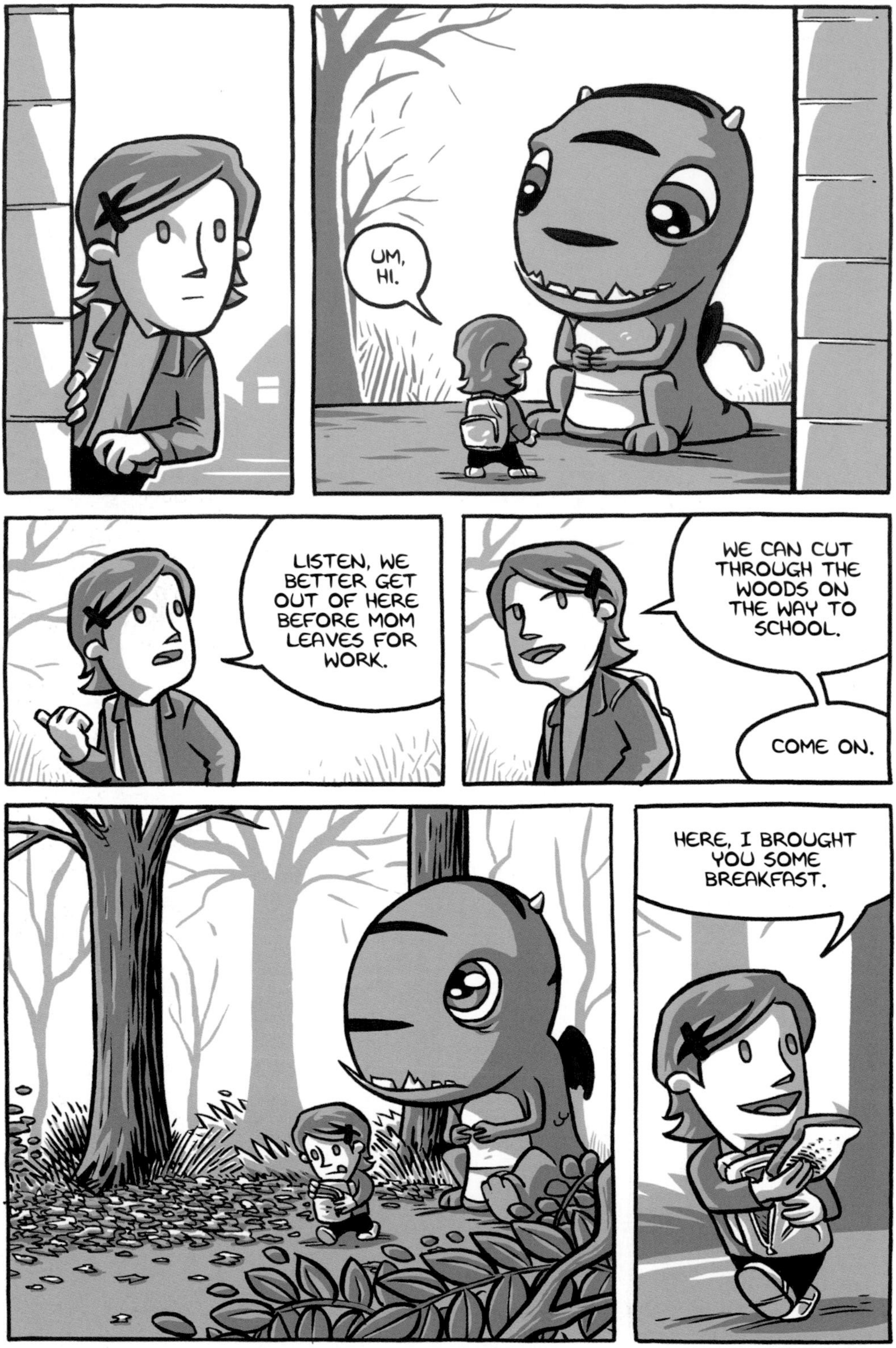
UM, HI.
LISTEN, WE BETTER GET OUT OF HERE BEFORE MOM LEAVES FOR WORK.
WE CAN CUT THROUGH THE WOODS ON THE WAY TO SCHOOL.
COME ON.
HERE, I BROUGHT YOU SOME BREAKFAST.

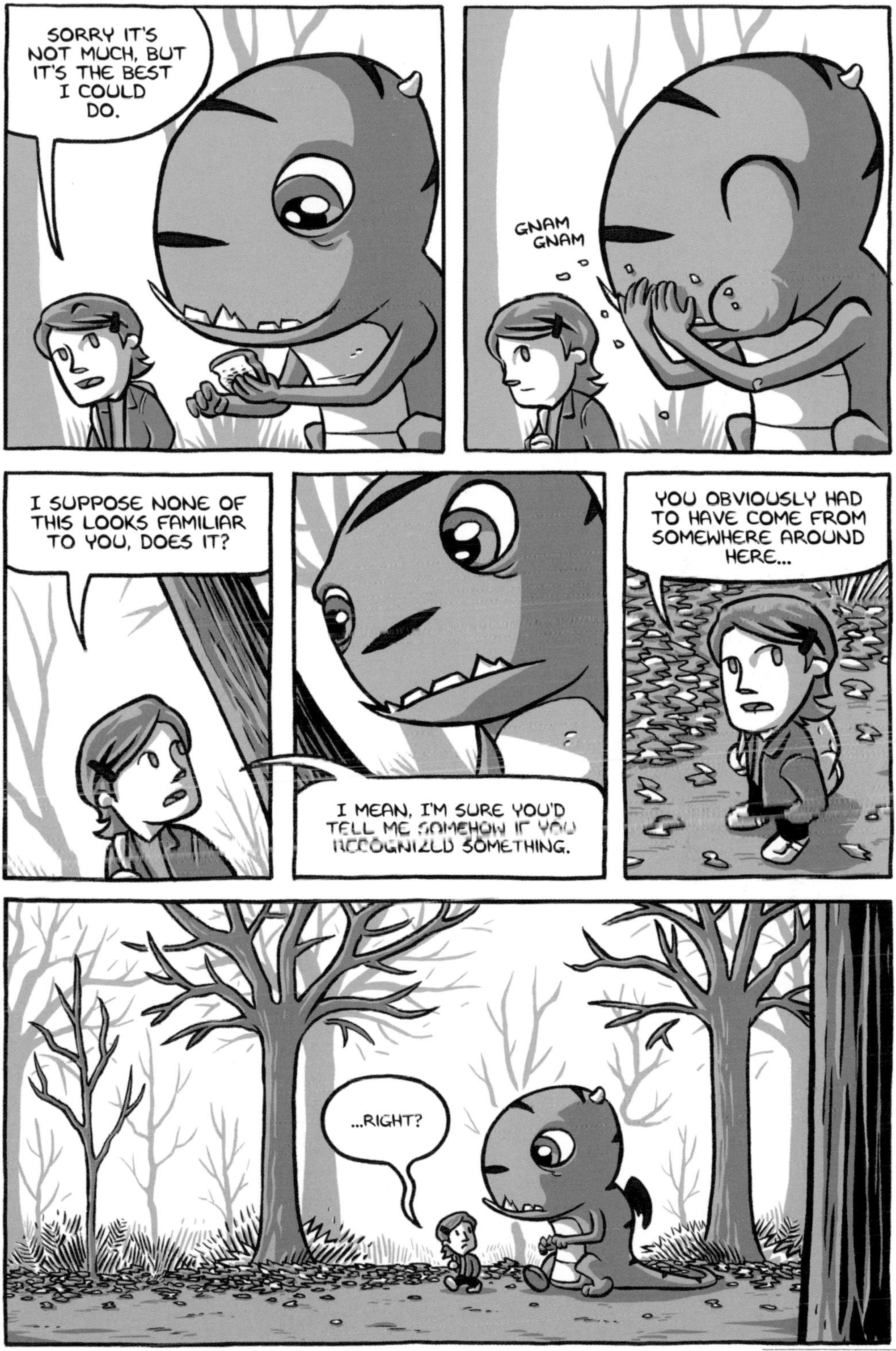
SORRY IT'S NOT MUCH, BUT IT'S THE BEST I COULD DO.
GNAM GNAM
I SUPPOSE NONE OF THIS LOOKS FAMILIAR TO YOU, DOES IT?
I MEAN, I'M SURE YOU'D TELL ME SOMEHOW IF YOU RECOGNIZED SOMETHING.
YOU OBVIOUSLY HAD TO HAVE COME FROM SOMEWHERE AROUND HERE...
...RIGHT?

48

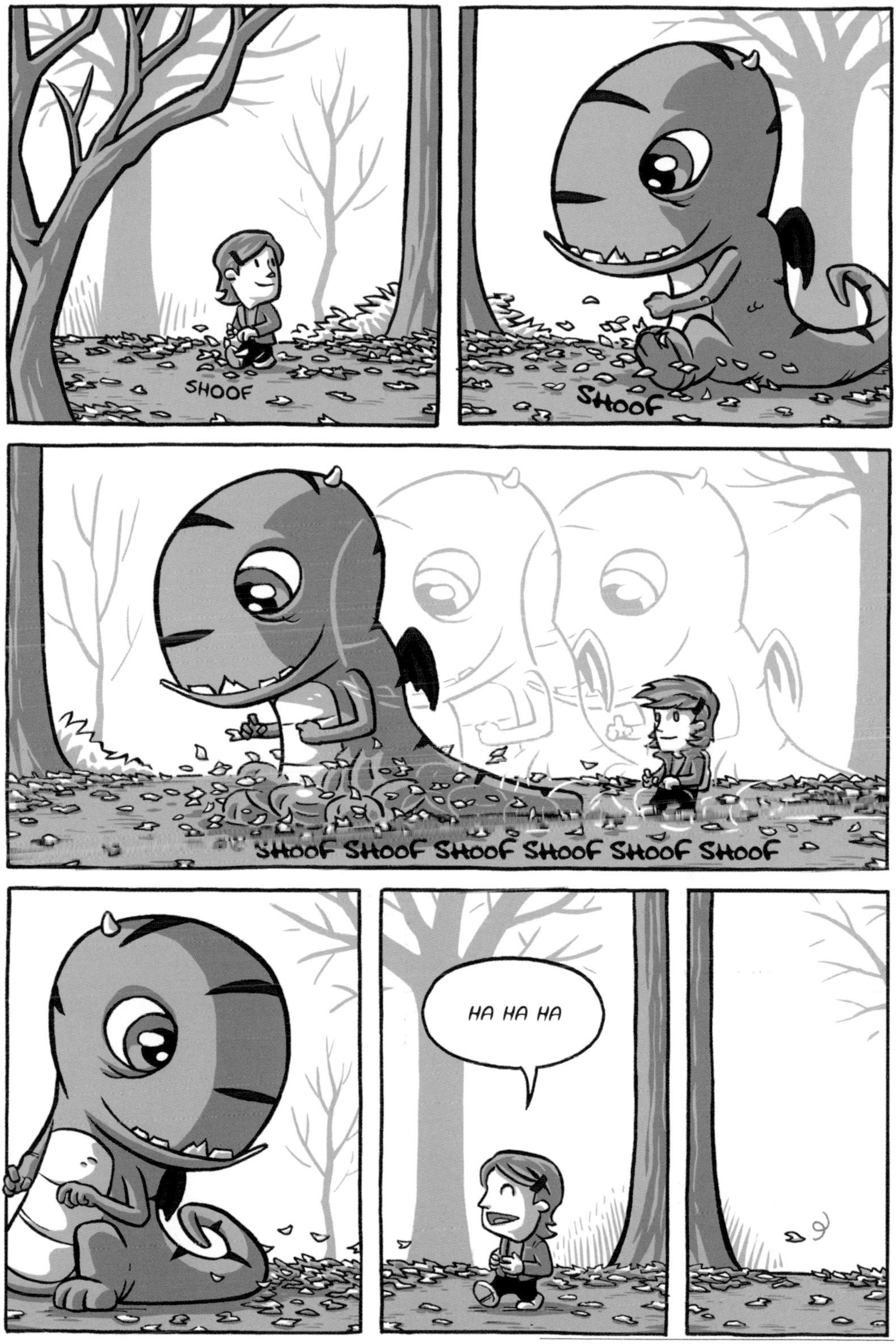
SHOOF
SHOOF
SHOOF SHOOF SHOOF SHOOF SHOOF SHOOF
HA HA HA

50

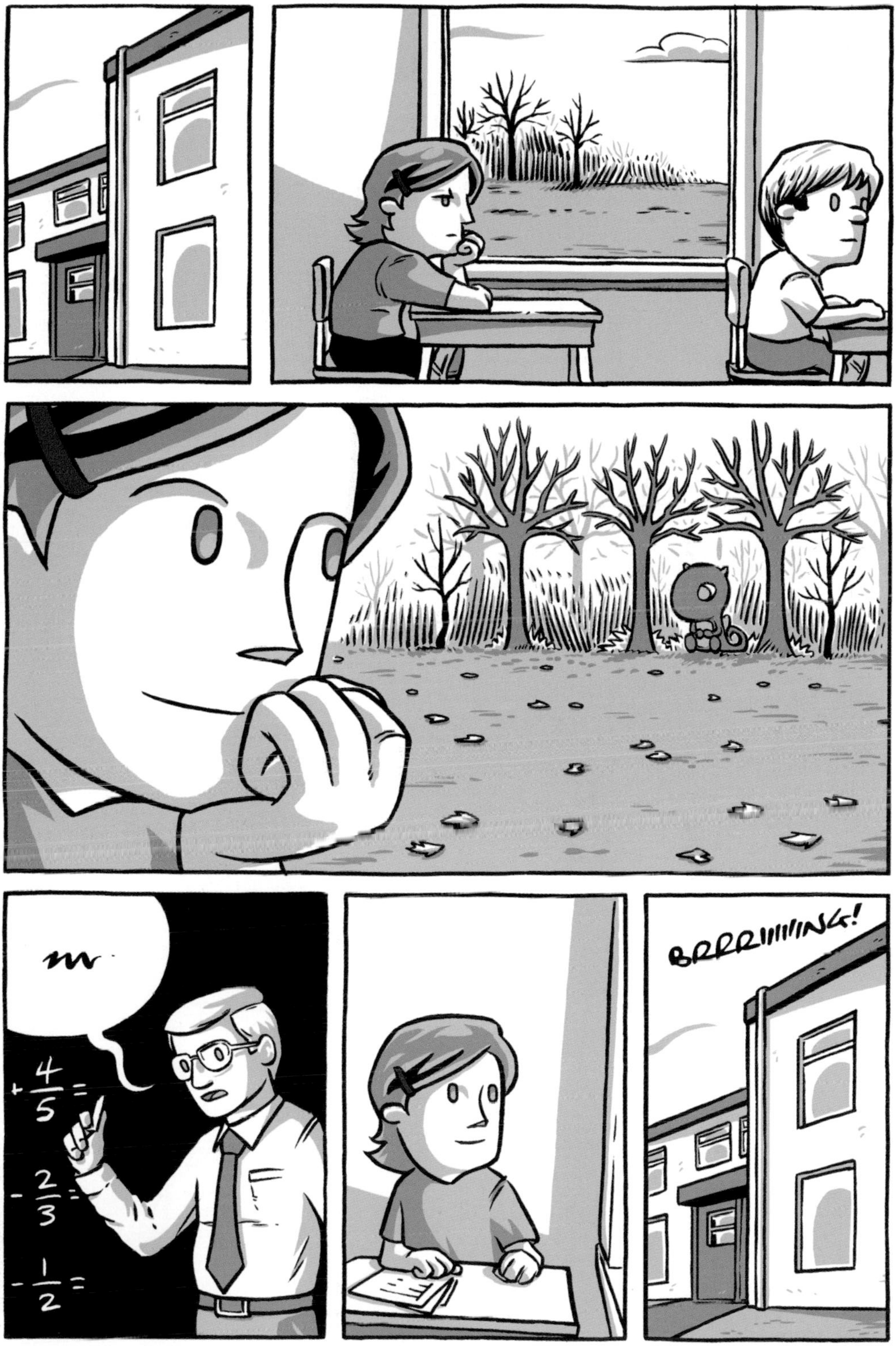
+ 4/5 =
- 2/3 =
- 1/2 =
BRRRIIIIIIING!

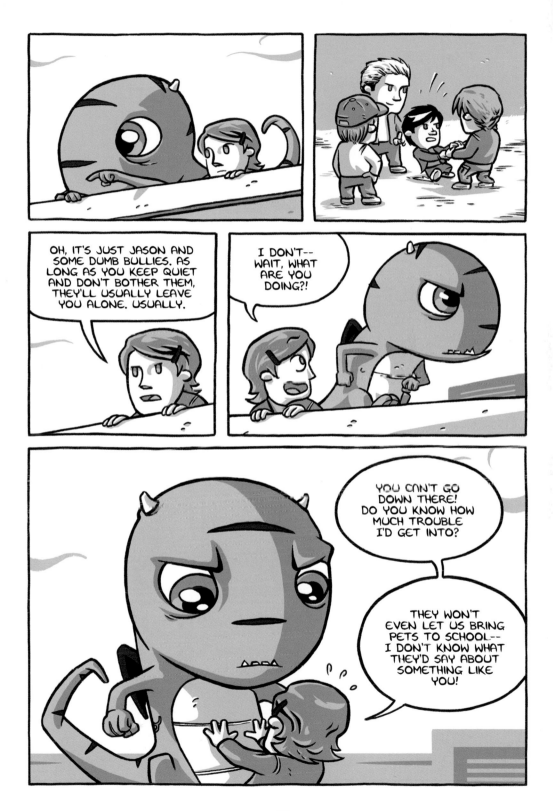

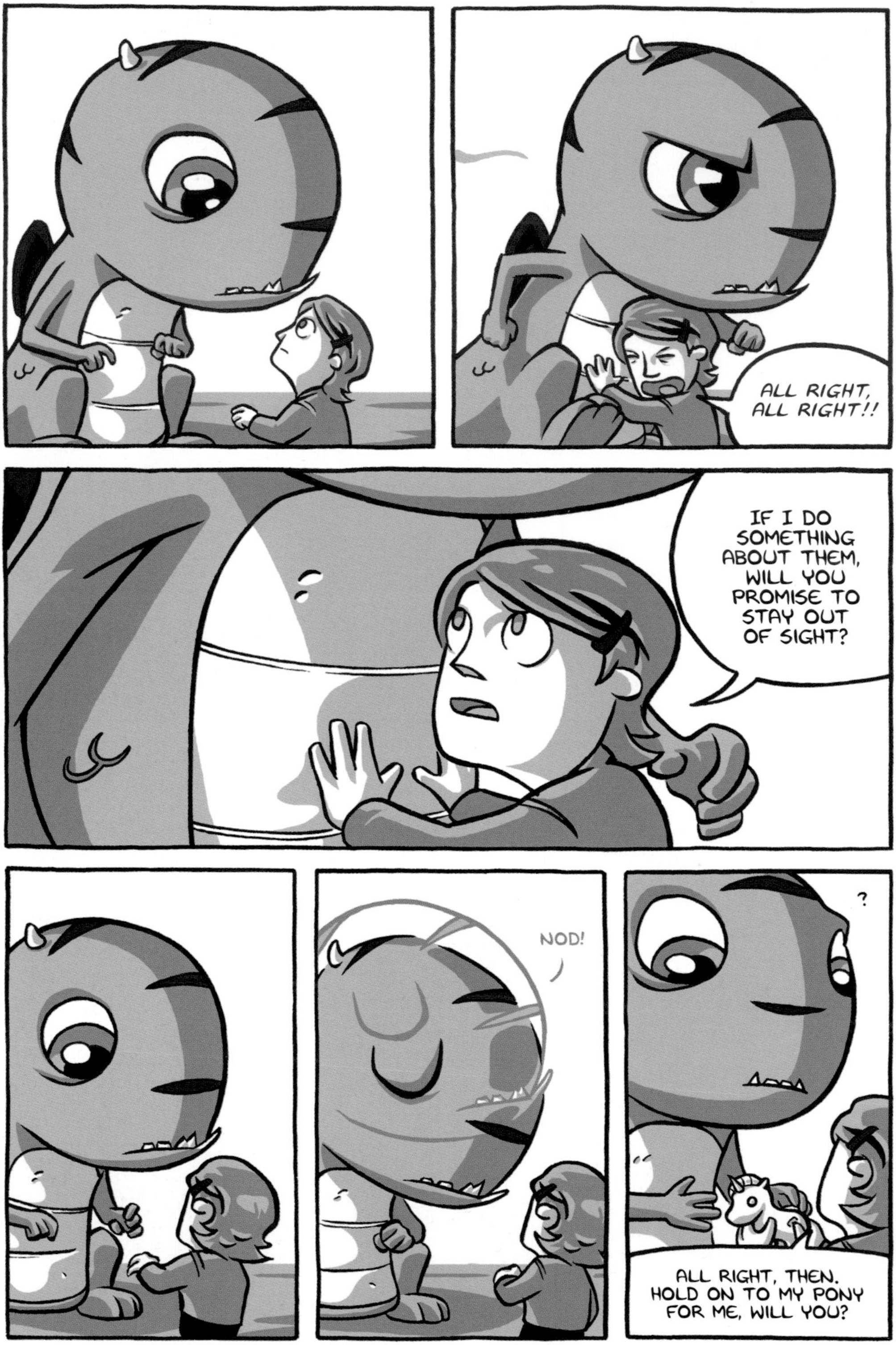
ALL RIGHT, ALL RIGHT!!
IF I DO SOMETHING ABOUT THEM, WILL YOU PROMISE TO STAY OUT OF SIGHT?
NOD!
?
ALL RIGHT, THEN. HOLD ON TO MY PONY FOR ME, WILL YOU?

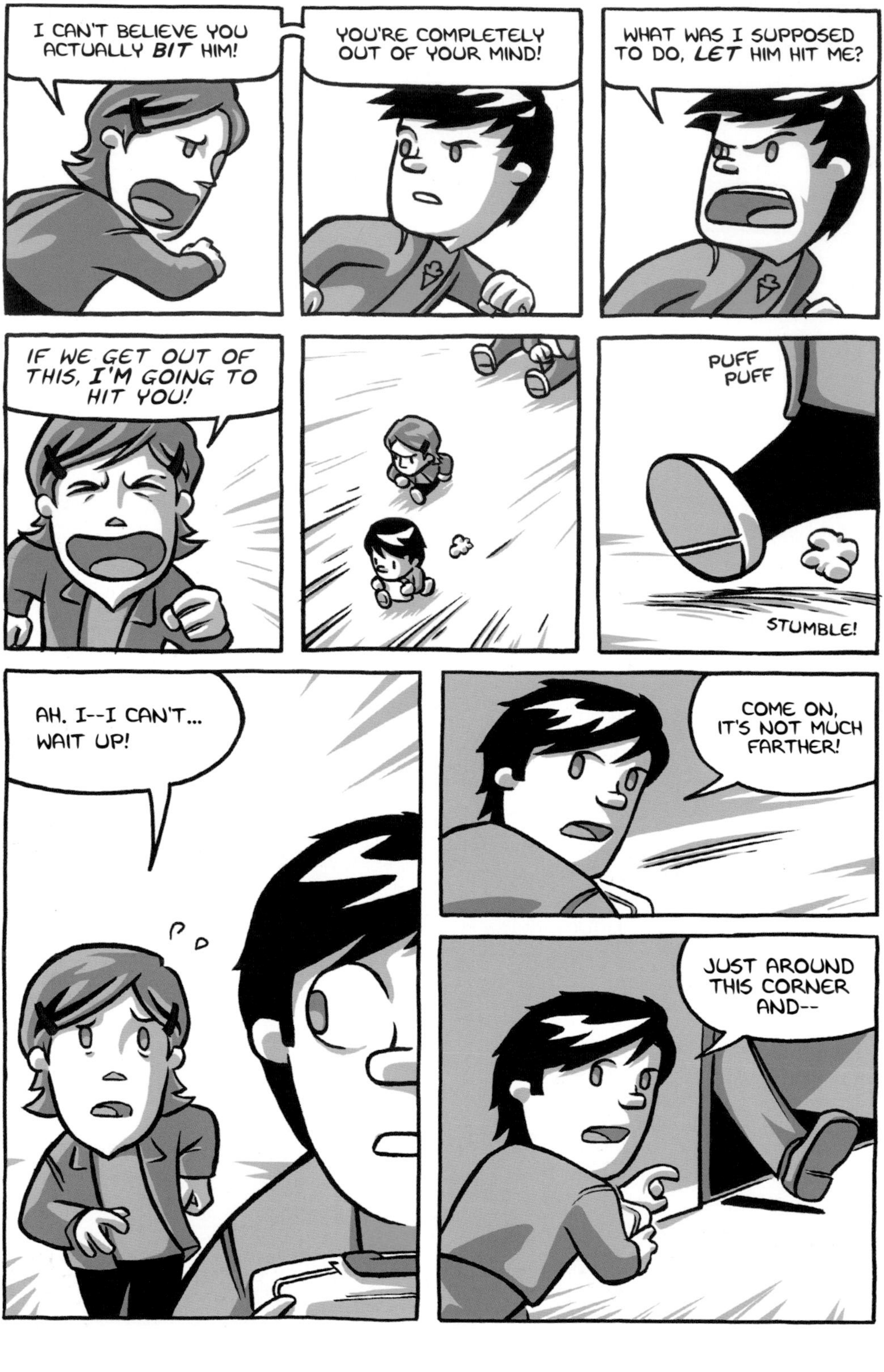
I CAN'T BELIEVE YOU ACTUALLY BIT HIM!
YOU'RE COMPLETELY OUT OF YOUR MIND!
WHAT WAS I SUPPOSED TO DO, LET HIM HIT ME?
IF WE GET OUT OF THIS, I'M GOING TO HIT YOU!
PUFF PUFF
STUMBLE!
AH. I--I CAN'T... WAIT UP!
COME ON, IT'S NOT MUCH FARTHER!
JUST AROUND THIS CORNER AND--

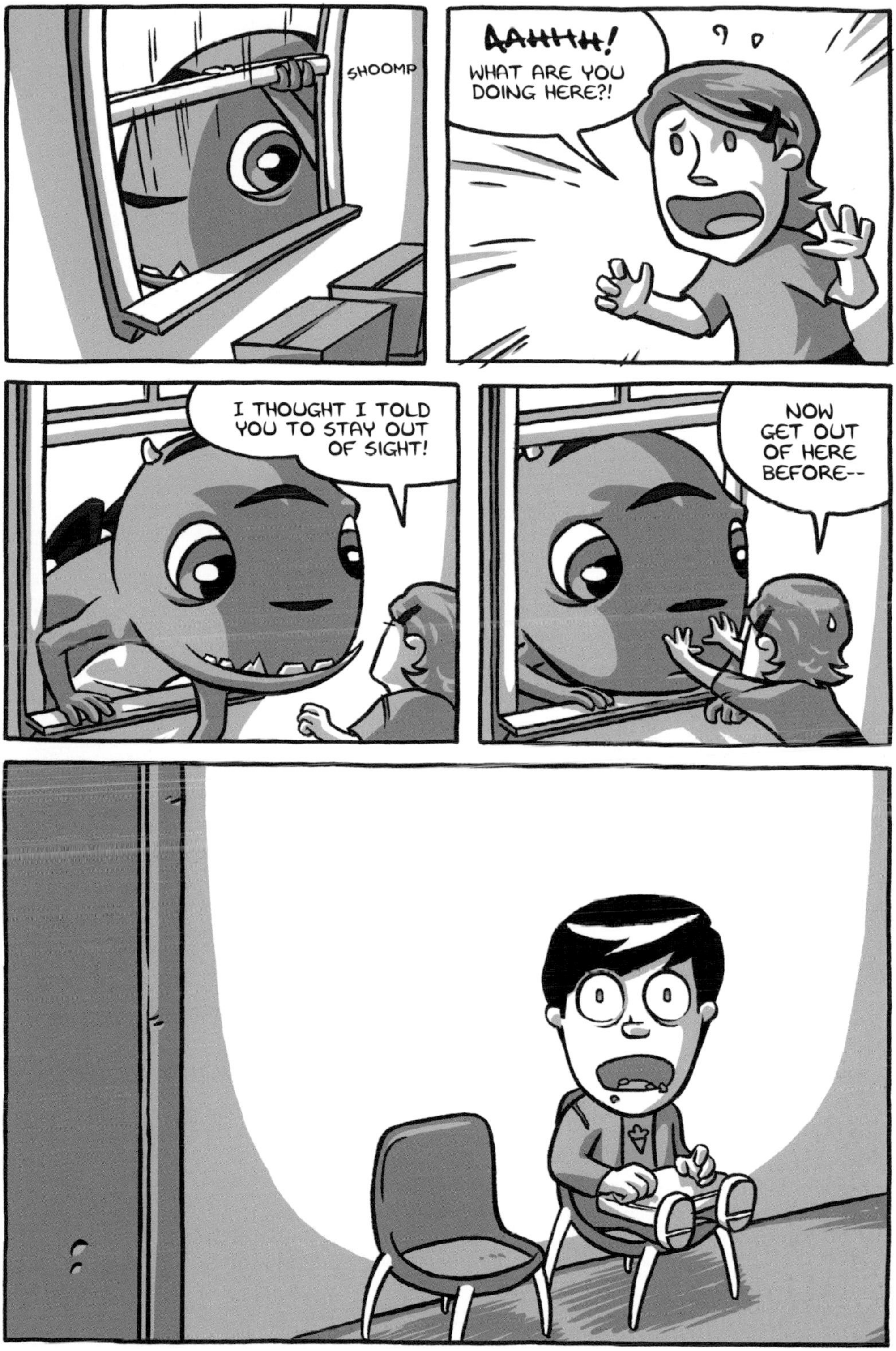
SHOOMP
AAHHH! WHAT ARE YOU DOING HERE?!
I THOUGHT I TOLD YOU TO STAY OUT OF SIGHT!
NOW GET OUT OF HERE BEFORE--

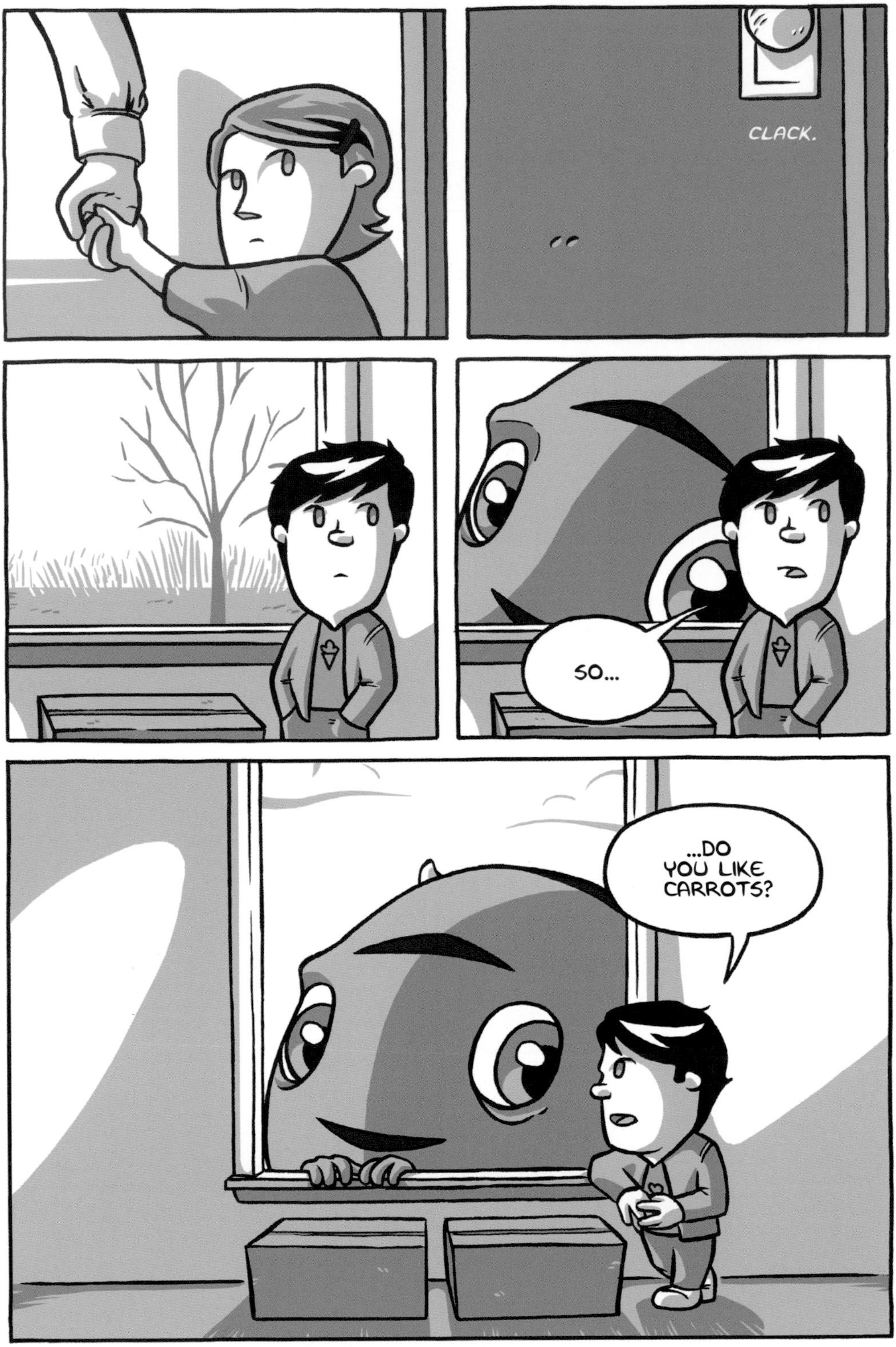
CLACK.
SO...
...DO YOU LIKE CARROTS?

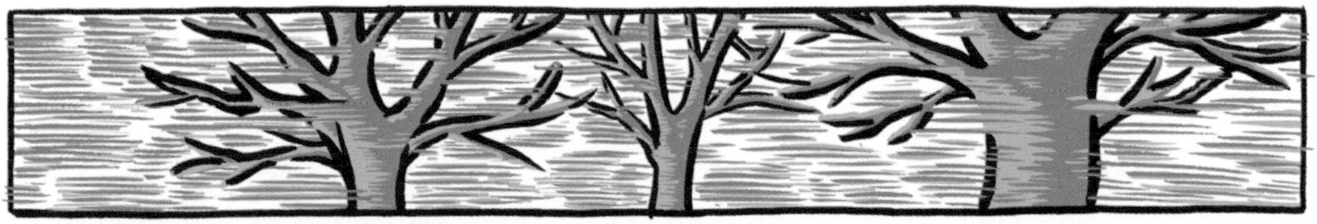

CHAPTER THREE

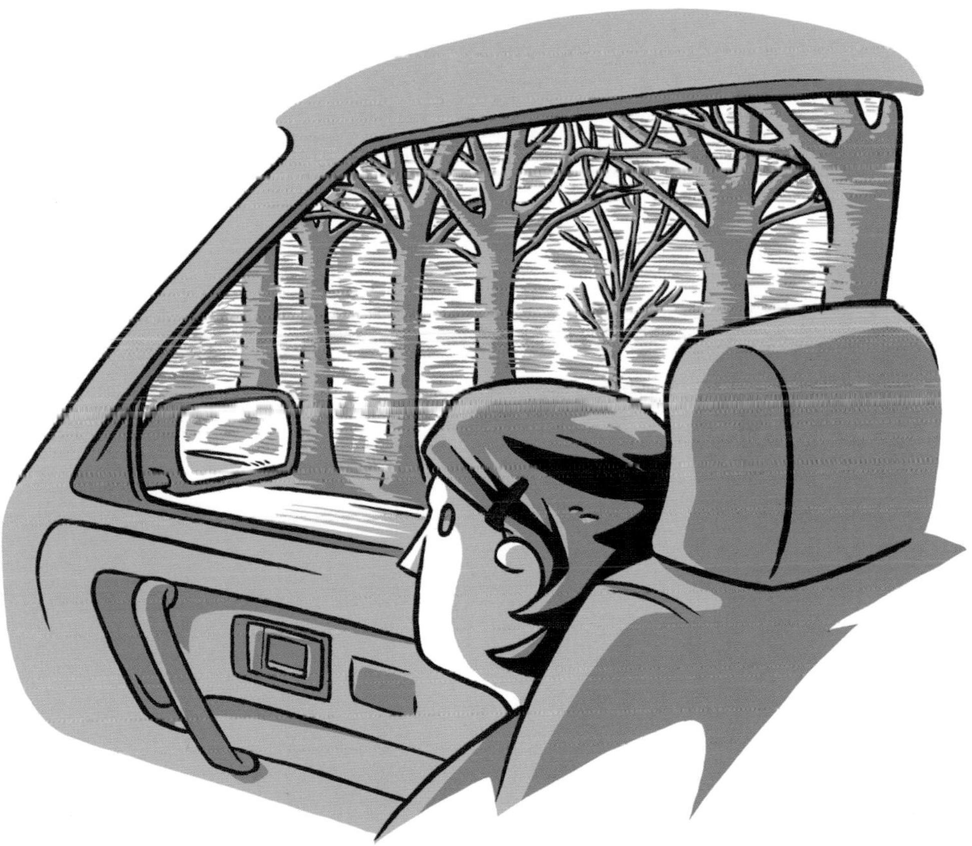

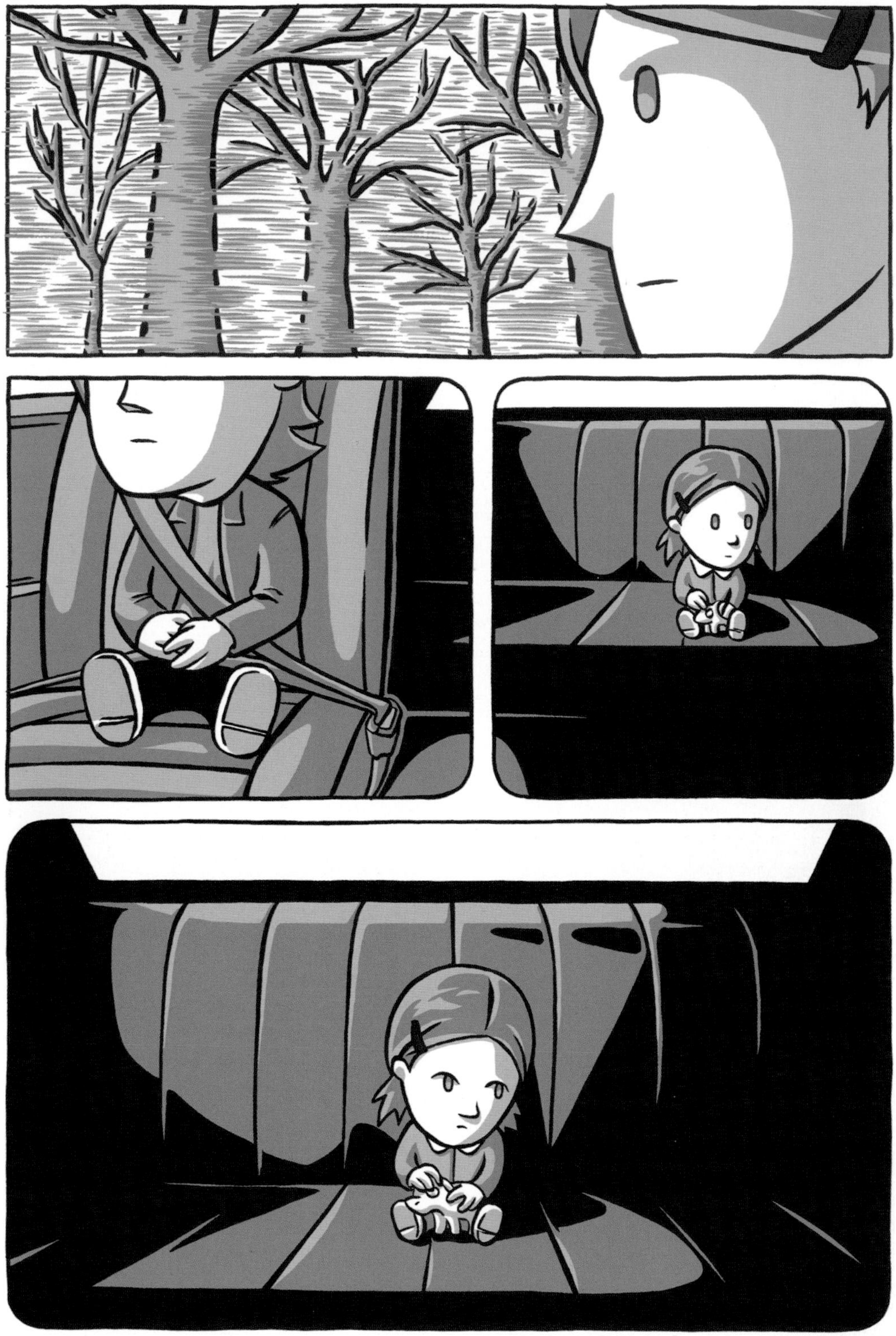

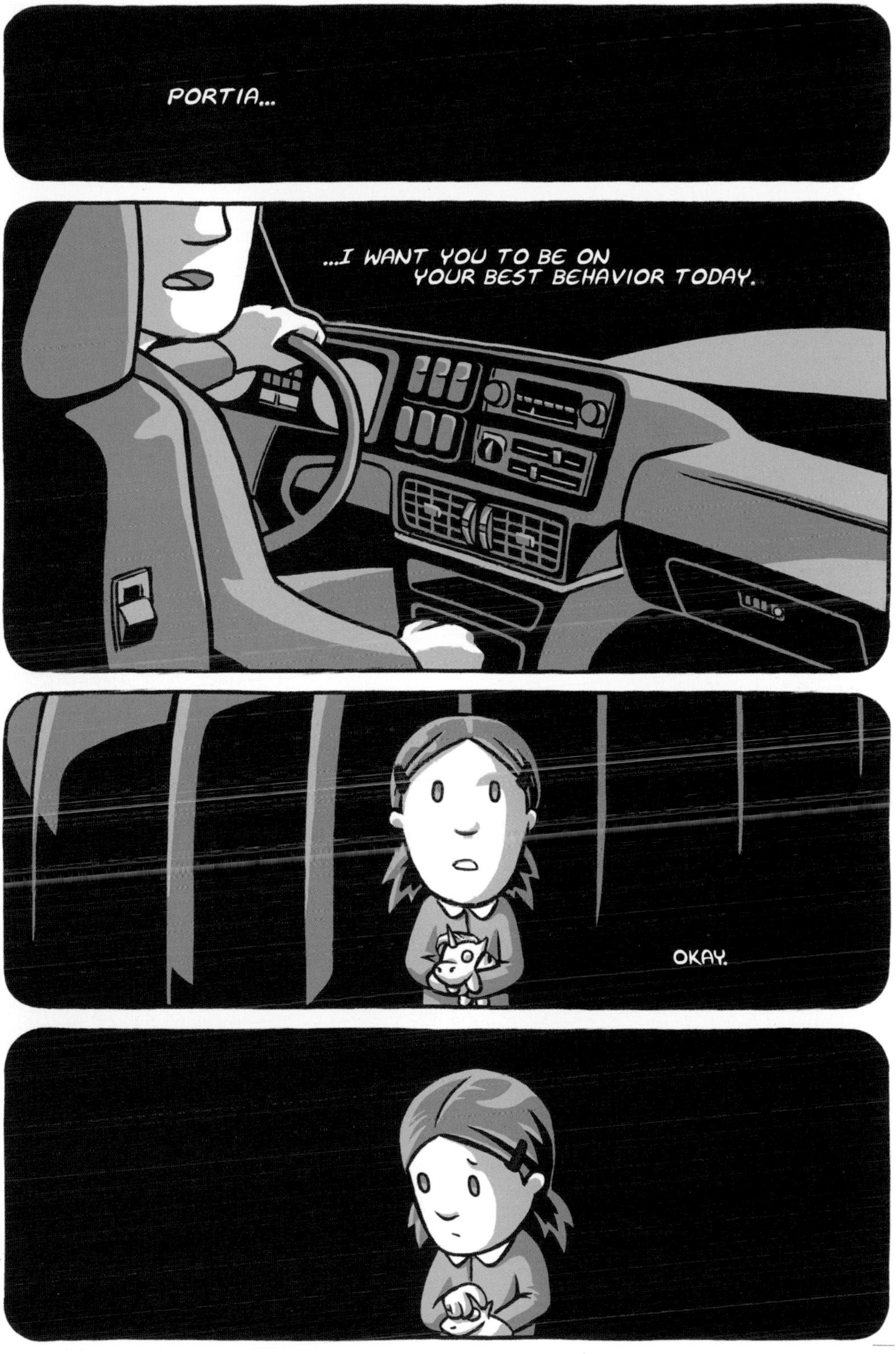
PORTIA...
...I WANT YOU TO BE ON YOUR BEST BEHAVIOR TODAY.
OKAY.

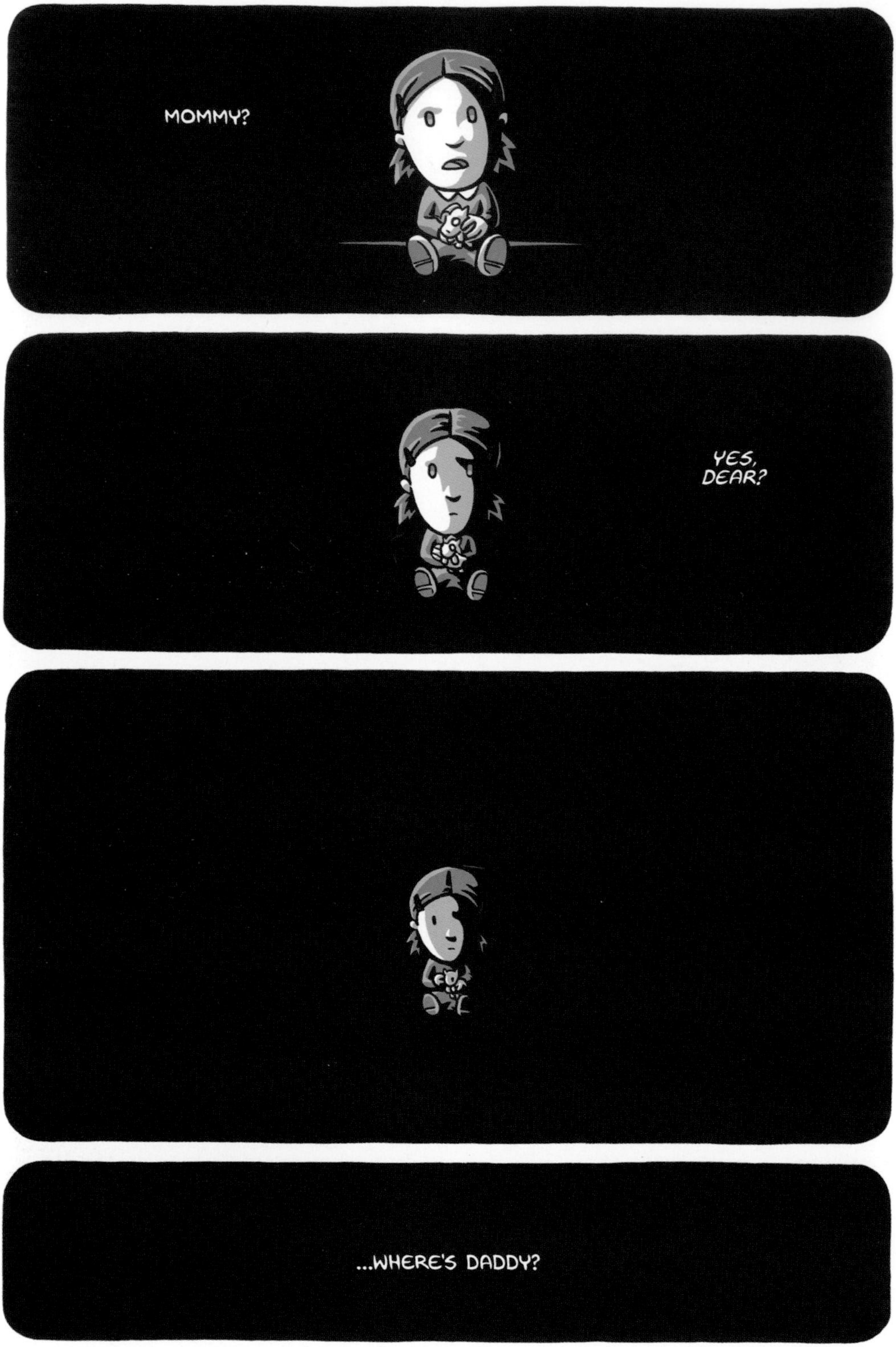
MOMMY?
YES, DEAR?
...WHERE'S DADDY?

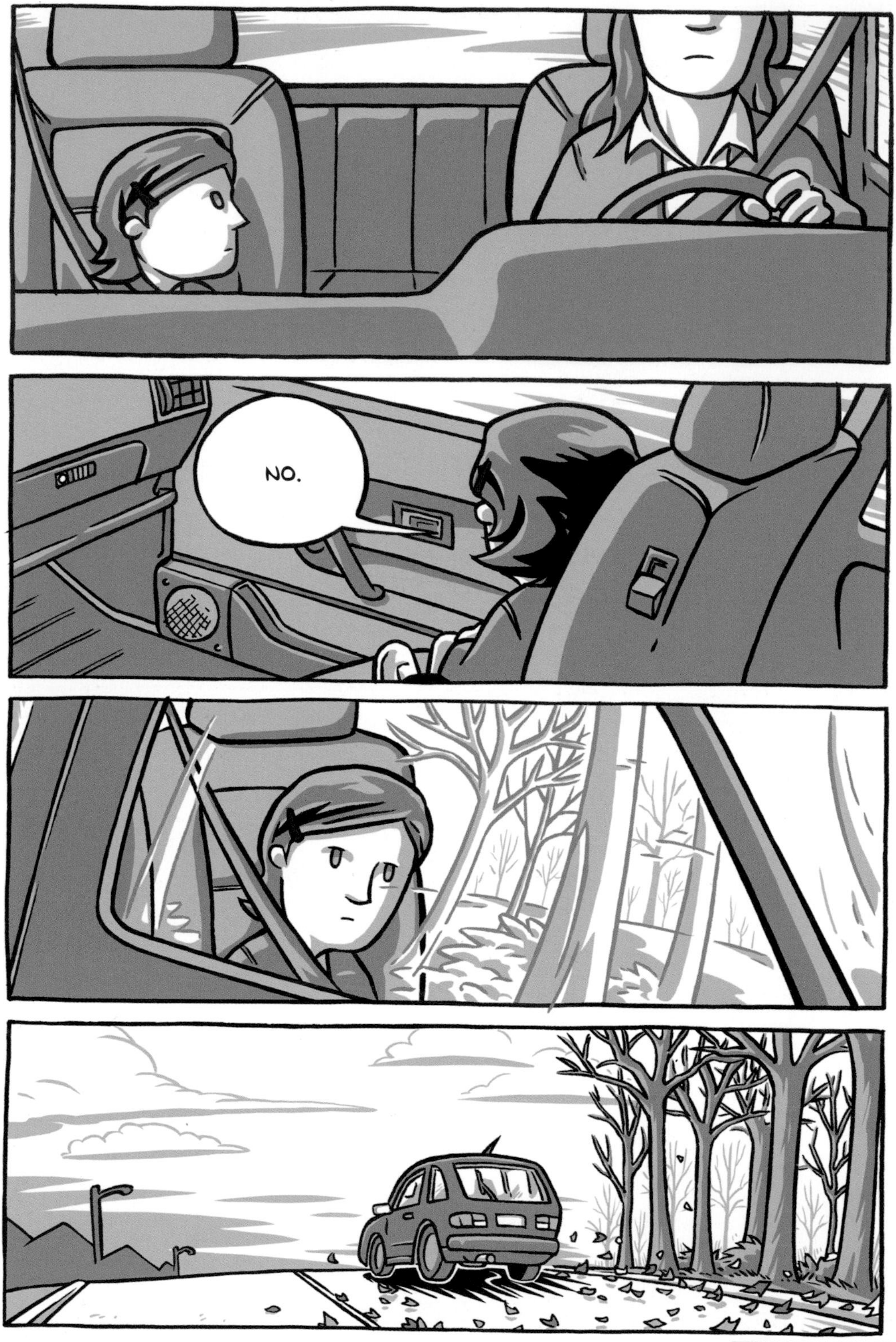
NO.

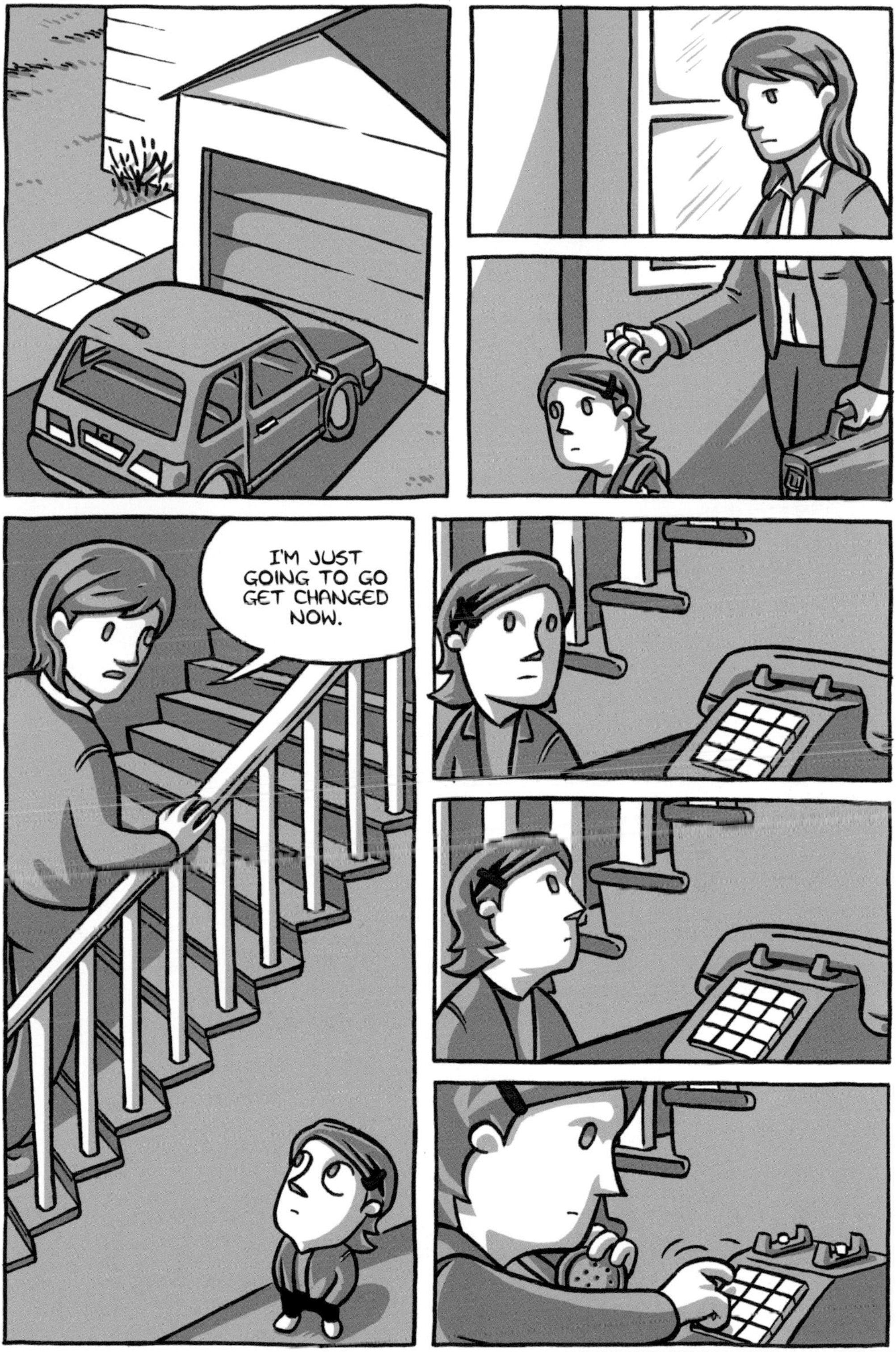
I'M JUST GOING TO GO GET CHANGED NOW.

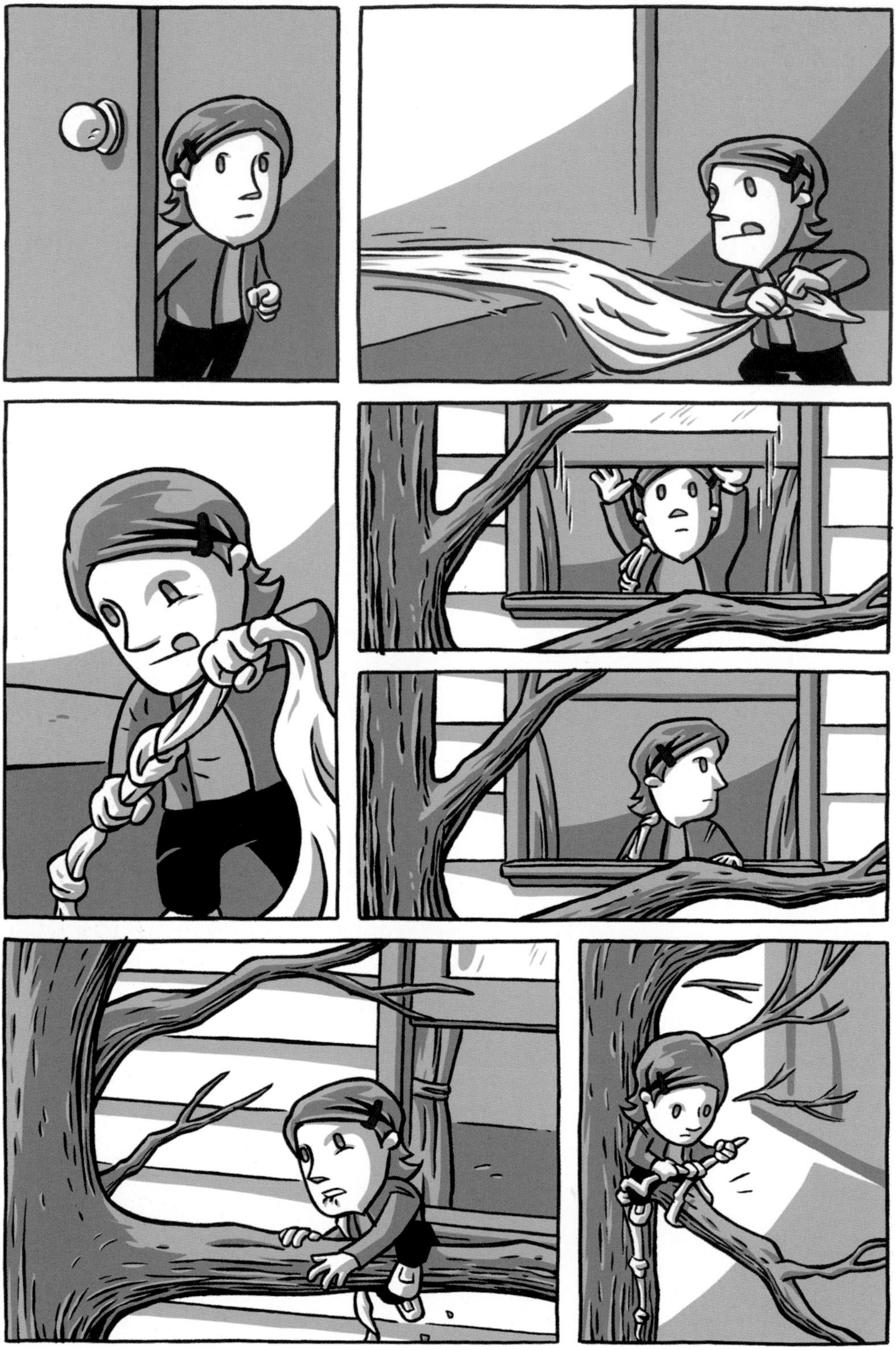

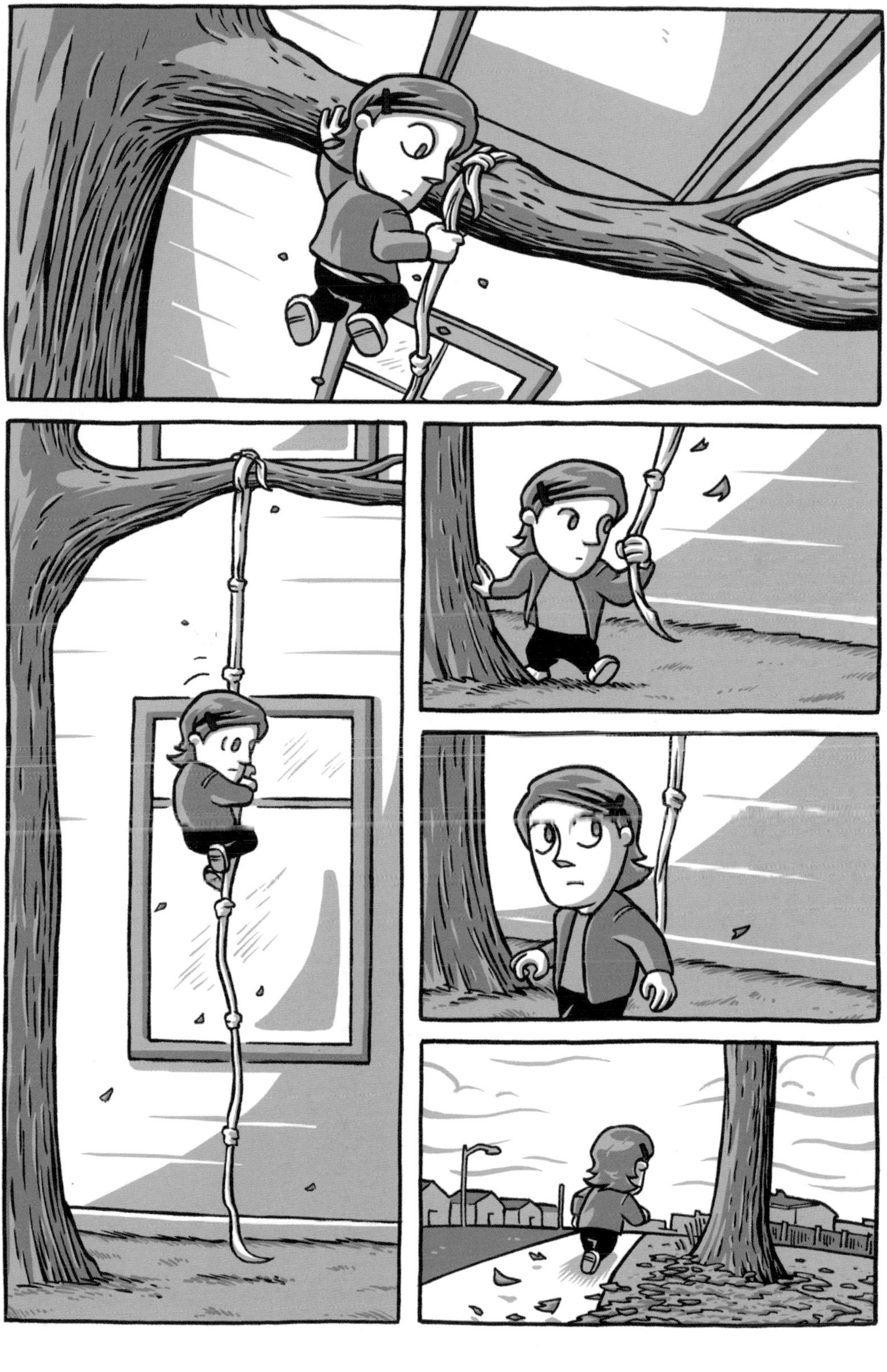

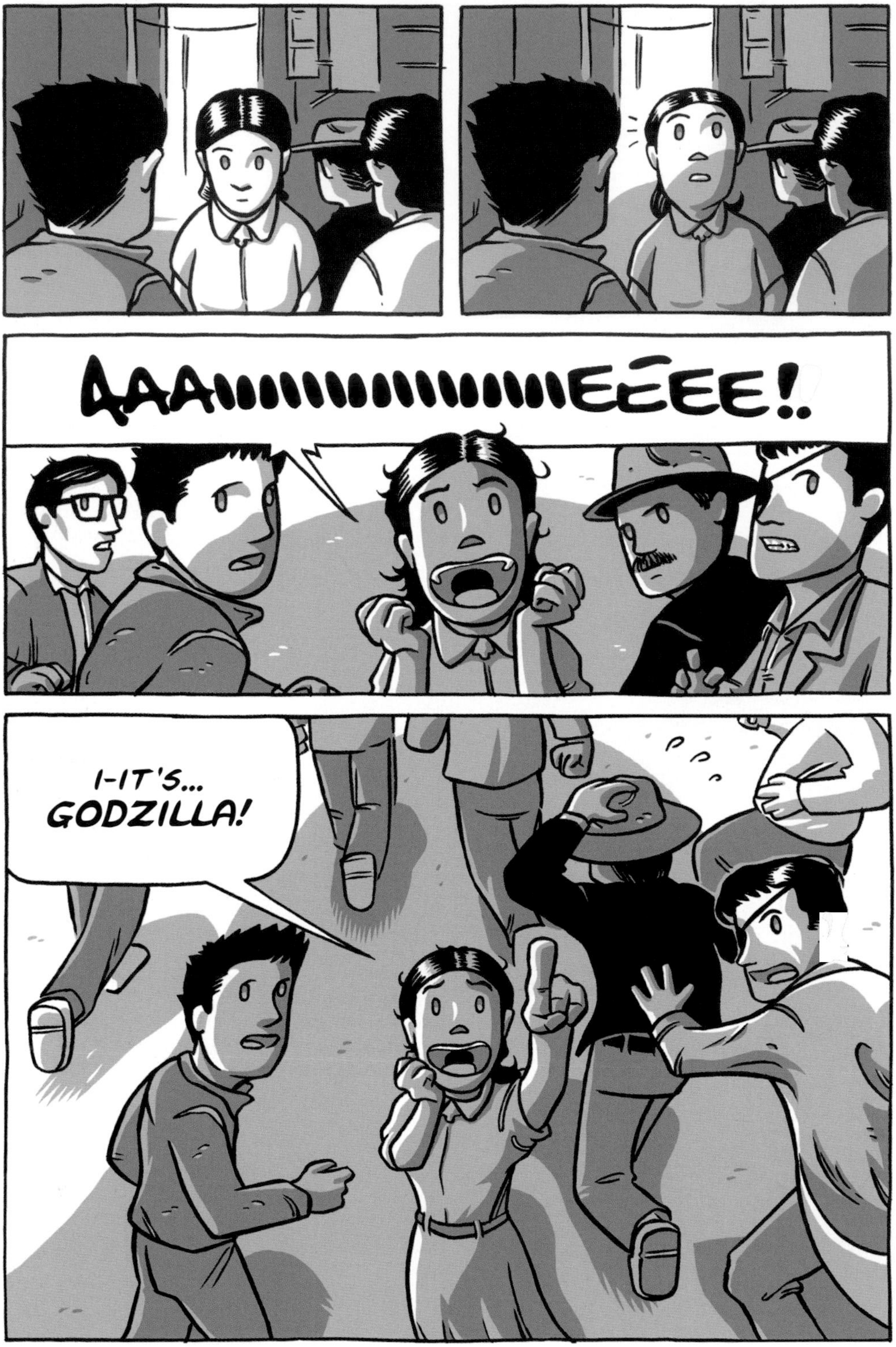
AAAIIIIIIIIIIIIIIIIIIEEEEE!!
I-IT'S... GODZILLA!

89

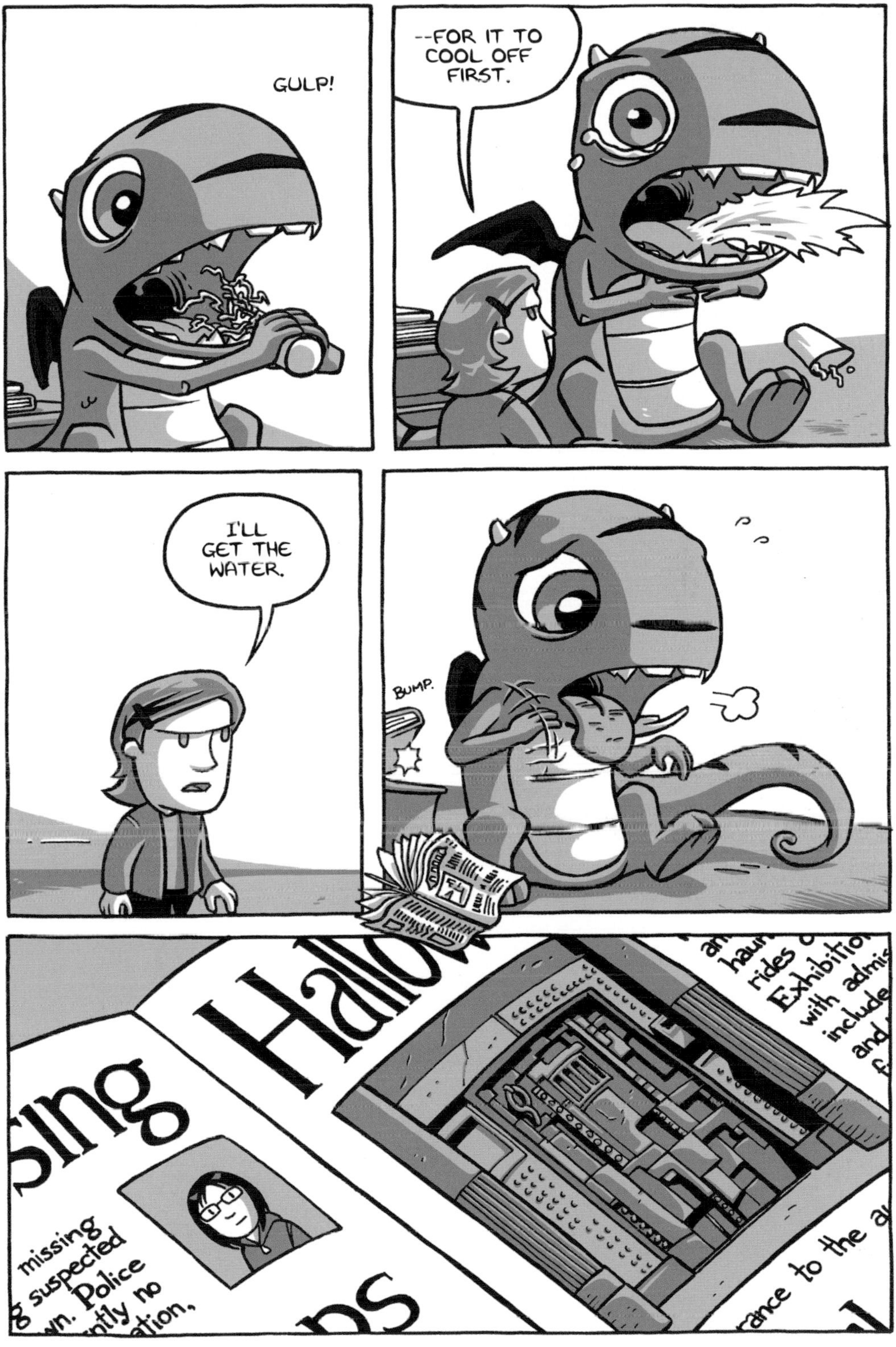
GULP!
--FOR IT TO COOL OFF FIRST.
I'LL GET THE WATER.
BUMP.
missing
suspected
Police
ntly no
ation,
Hallo
rides
Exhibitio
with admi
include
and
rance to the a

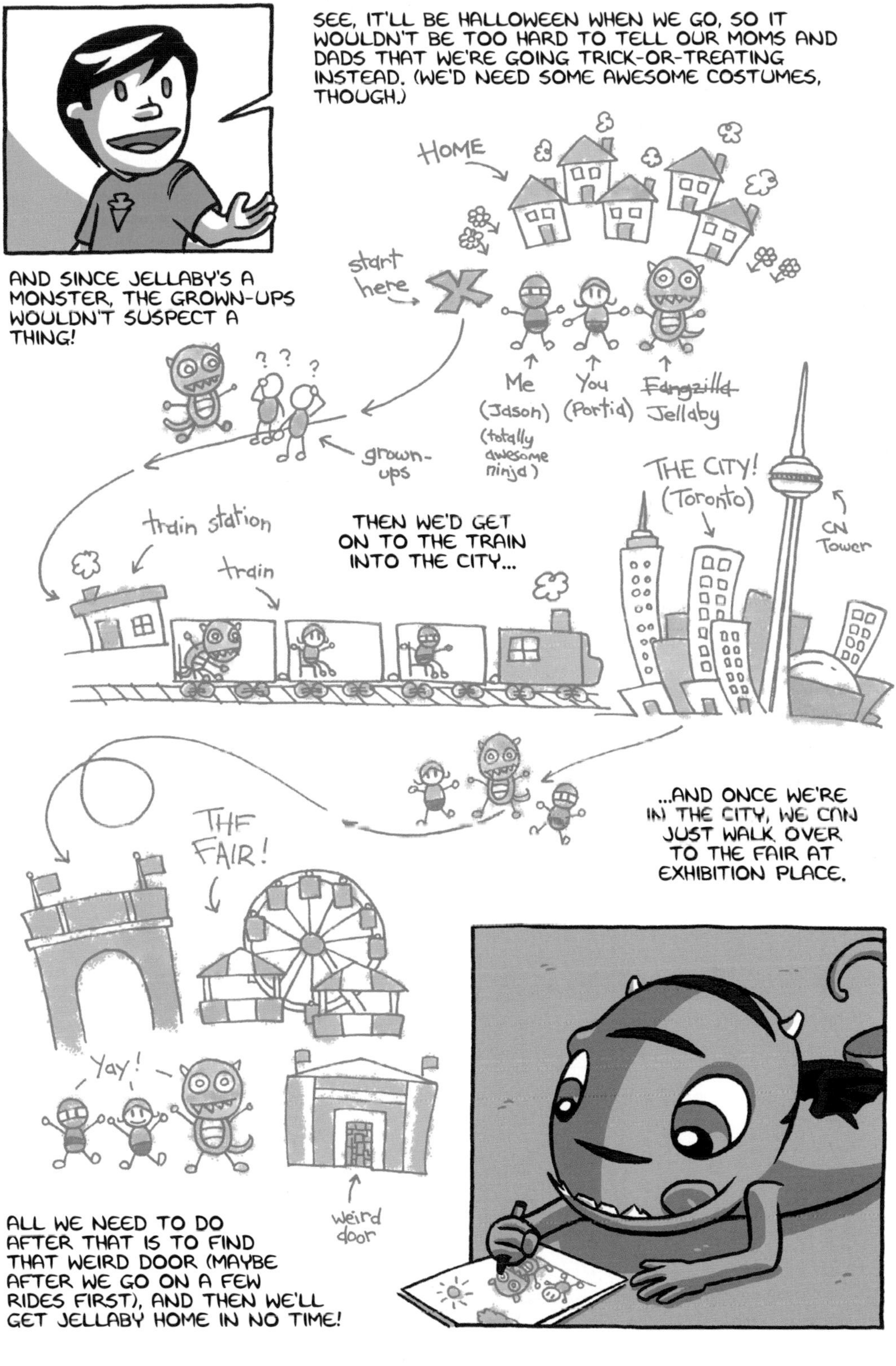

SEE, IT'LL BE HALLOWEEN WHEN WE GO, SO IT WOULDN'T BE TOO HARD TO TELL OUR MOMS AND DADS THAT WE'RE GOING TRICK-OR-TREATING INSTEAD. (WE'D NEED SOME AWESOME COSTUMES, THOUGH.)
AND SINCE JELLABY'S A MONSTER, THE GROWN-UPS WOULDN'T SUSPECT A THING!
HOME
start here
Me (Jason) (totally awesome ninja)
You (Portia)
~~Fangzilla~~ Jellaby
? ? ?
grown-ups
THE CITY! (Toronto)
CN Tower
train station
train
THEN WE'D GET ON TO THE TRAIN INTO THE CITY...
...AND ONCE WE'RE IN THE CITY, WE CAN JUST WALK OVER TO THE FAIR AT EXHIBITION PLACE.
THE FAIR!
Yay!
weird door
ALL WE NEED TO DO AFTER THAT IS TO FIND THAT WEIRD DOOR (MAYBE AFTER WE GO ON A FEW RIDES FIRST), AND THEN WE'LL GET JELLABY HOME IN NO TIME!

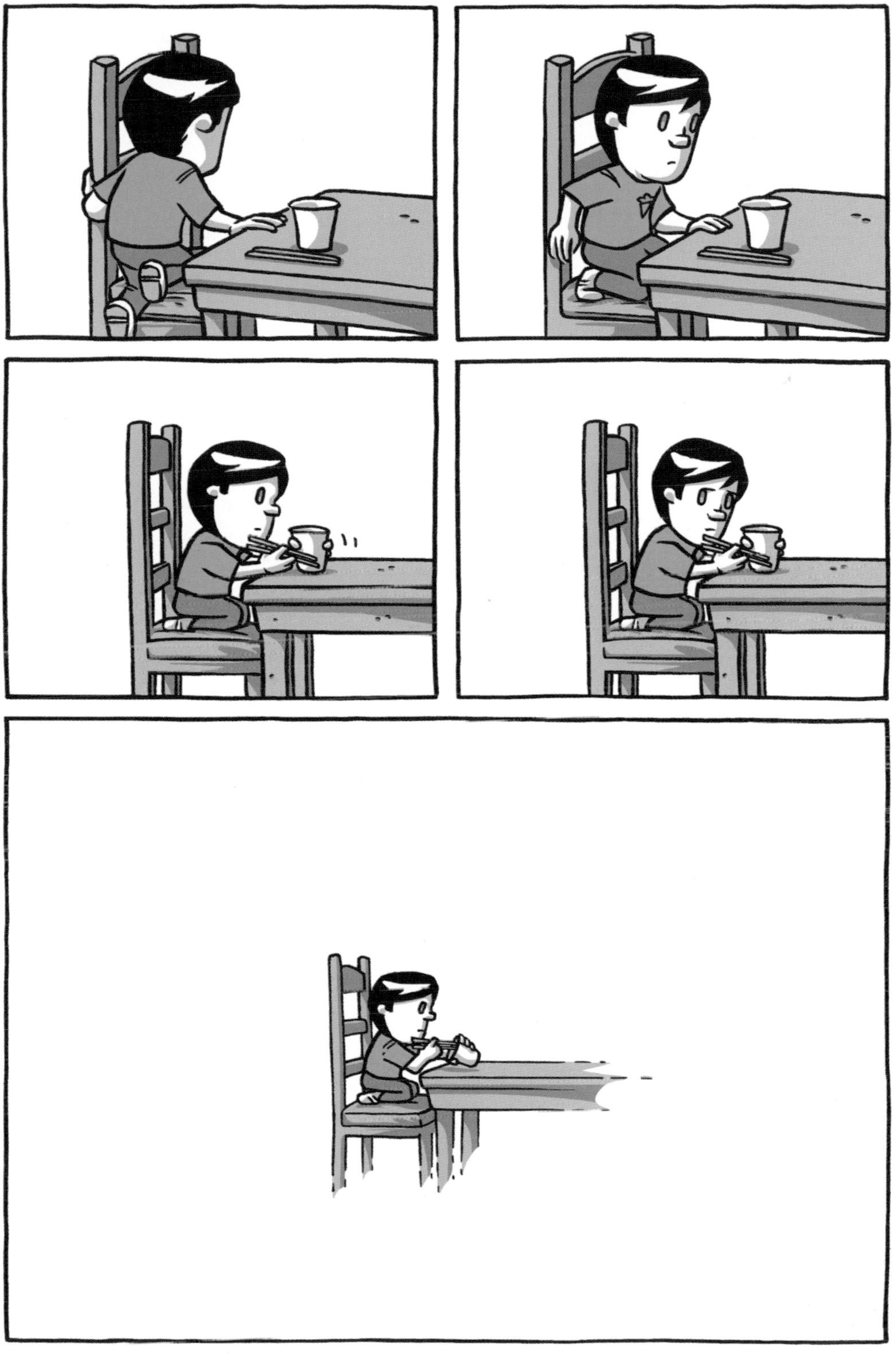

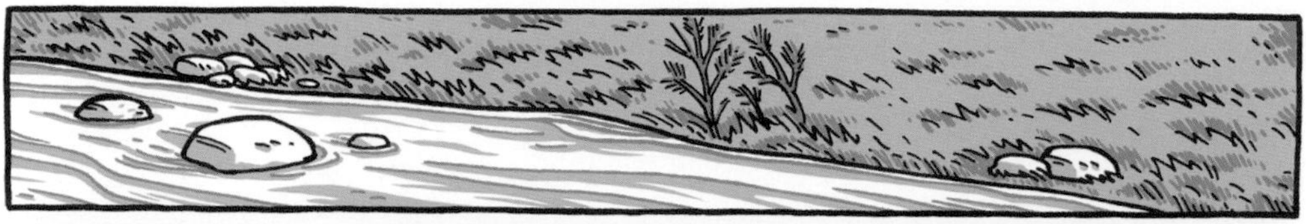

CHAPTER FOUR

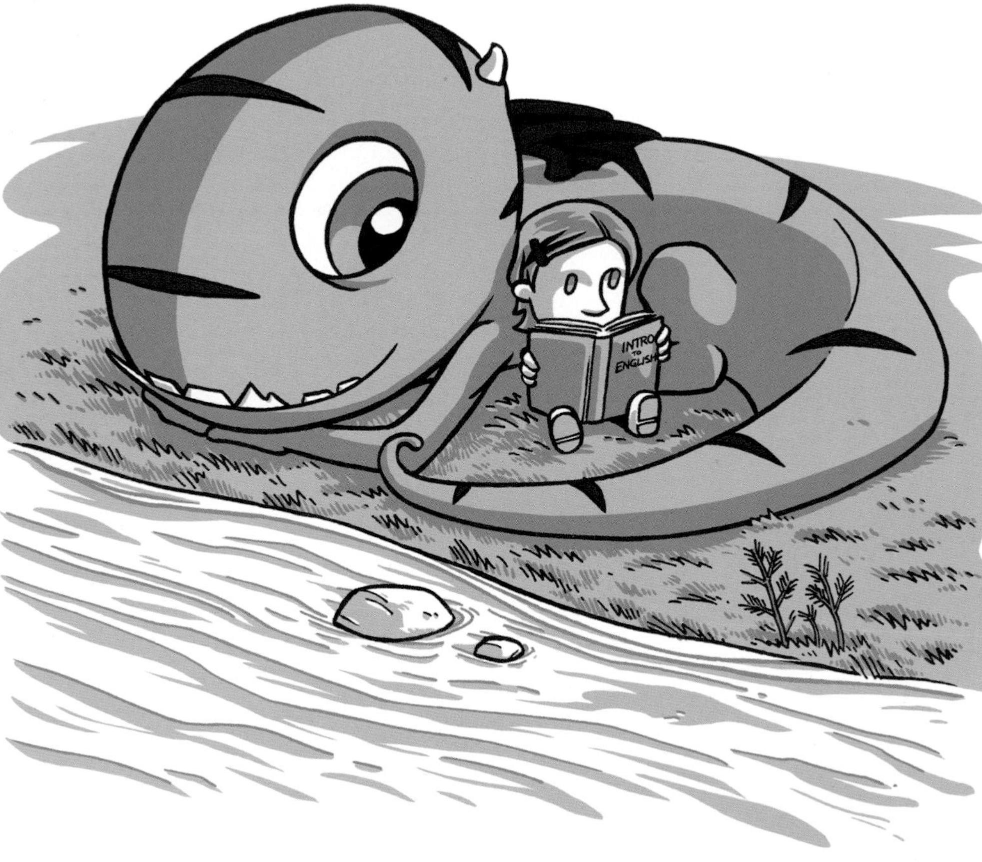
INTRO TO ENGLISH

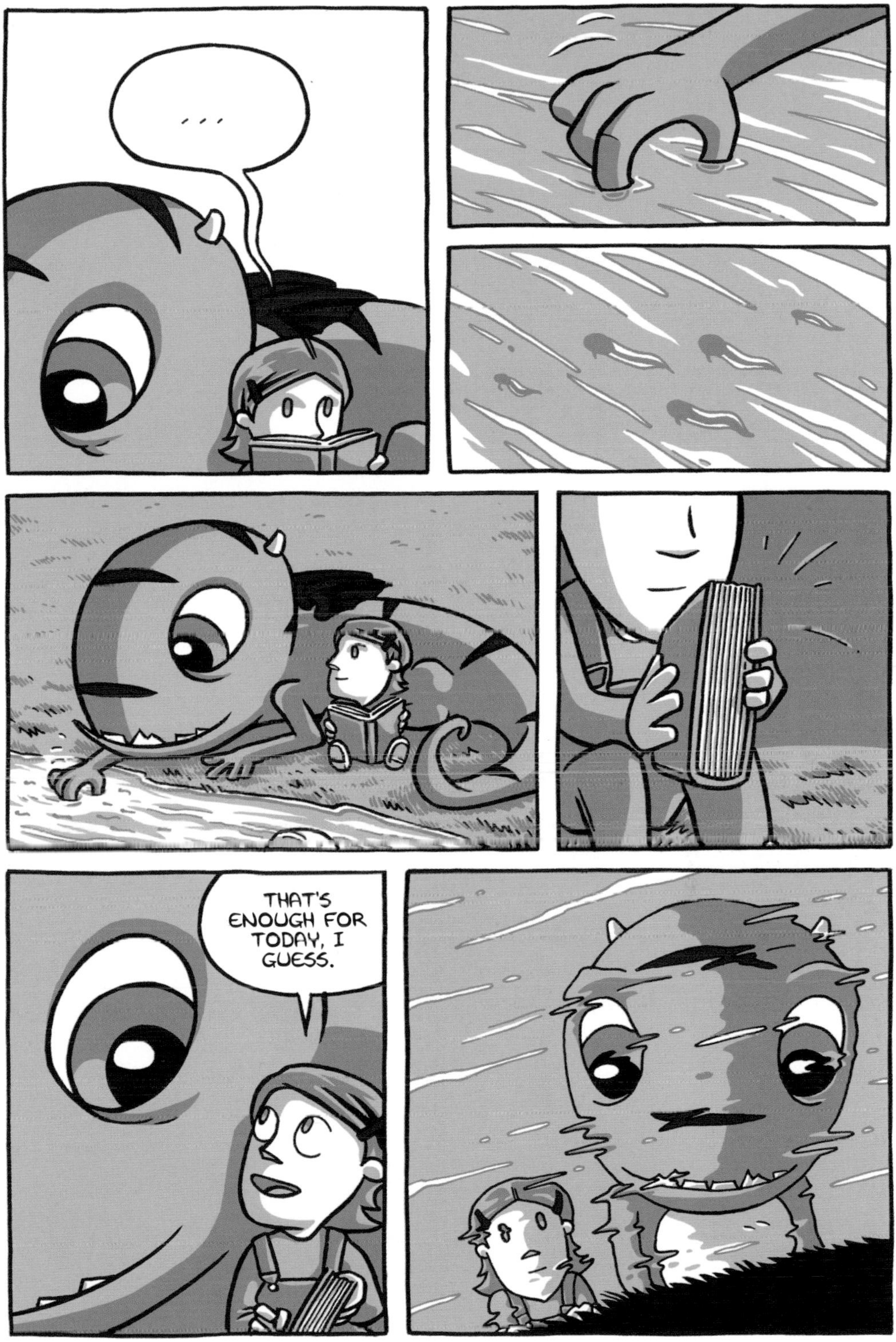
...
THAT'S ENOUGH FOR TODAY, I GUESS.

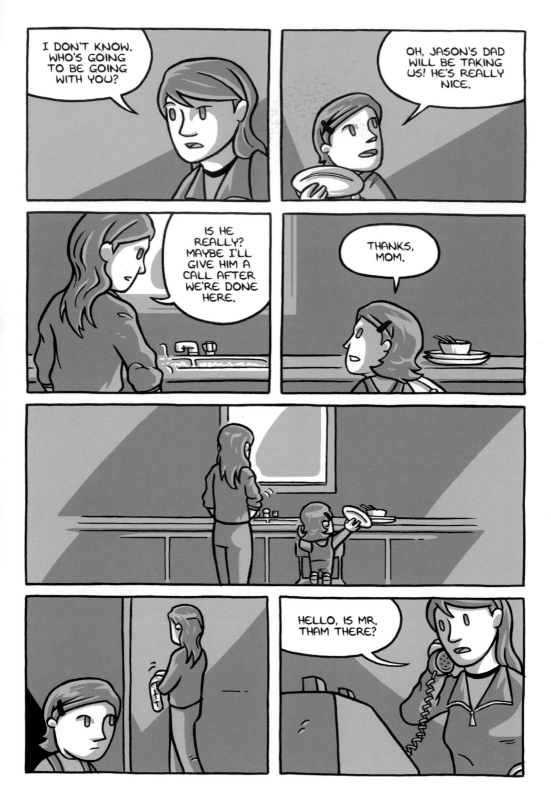

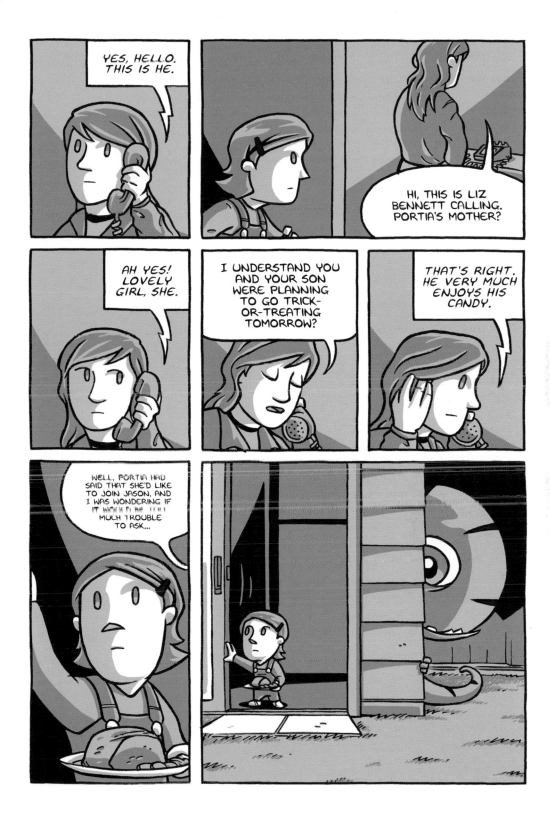

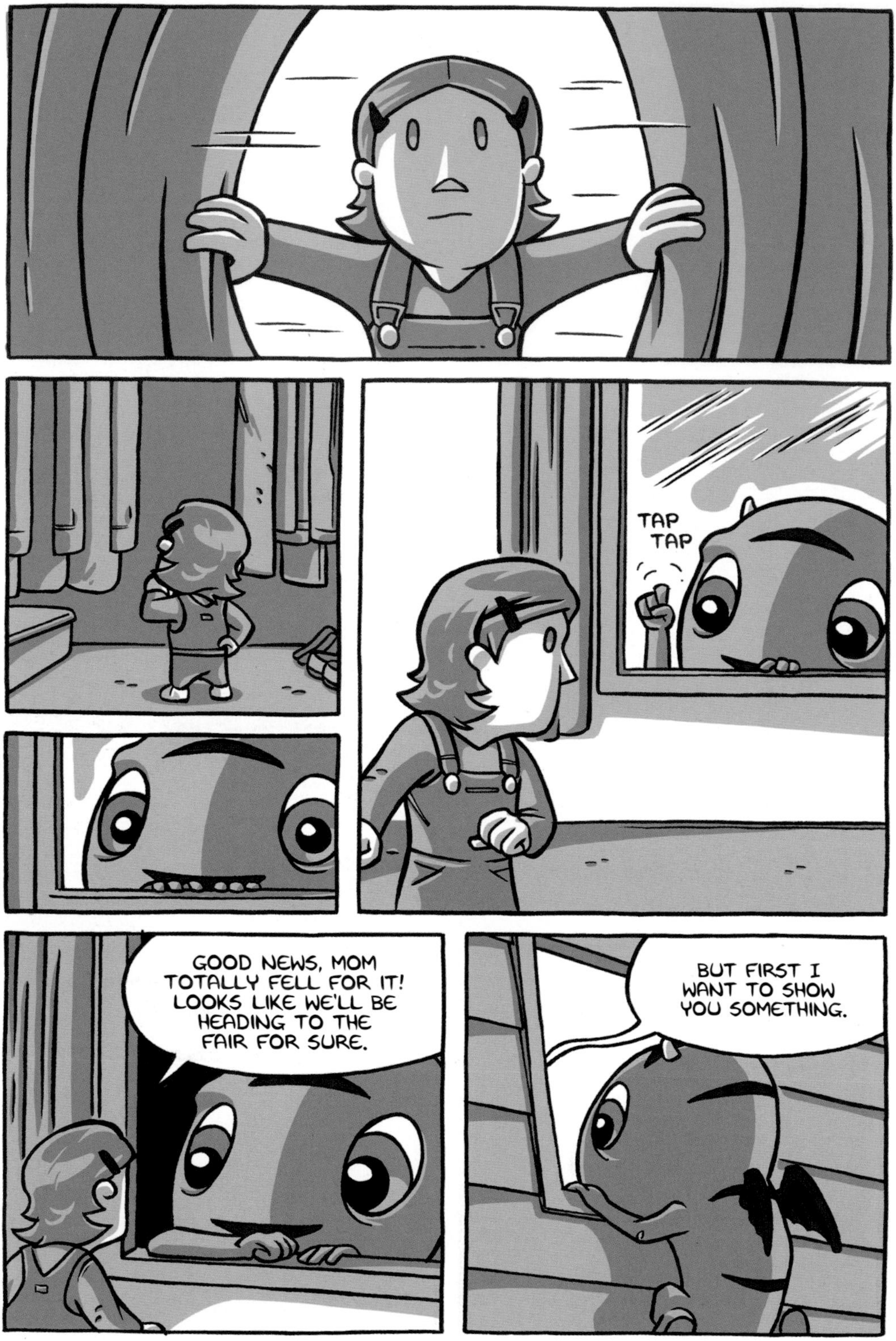
TAP
TAP
GOOD NEWS, MOM TOTALLY FELL FOR IT! LOOKS LIKE WE'LL BE HEADING TO THE FAIR FOR SURE.
BUT FIRST I WANT TO SHOW YOU SOMETHING.

111

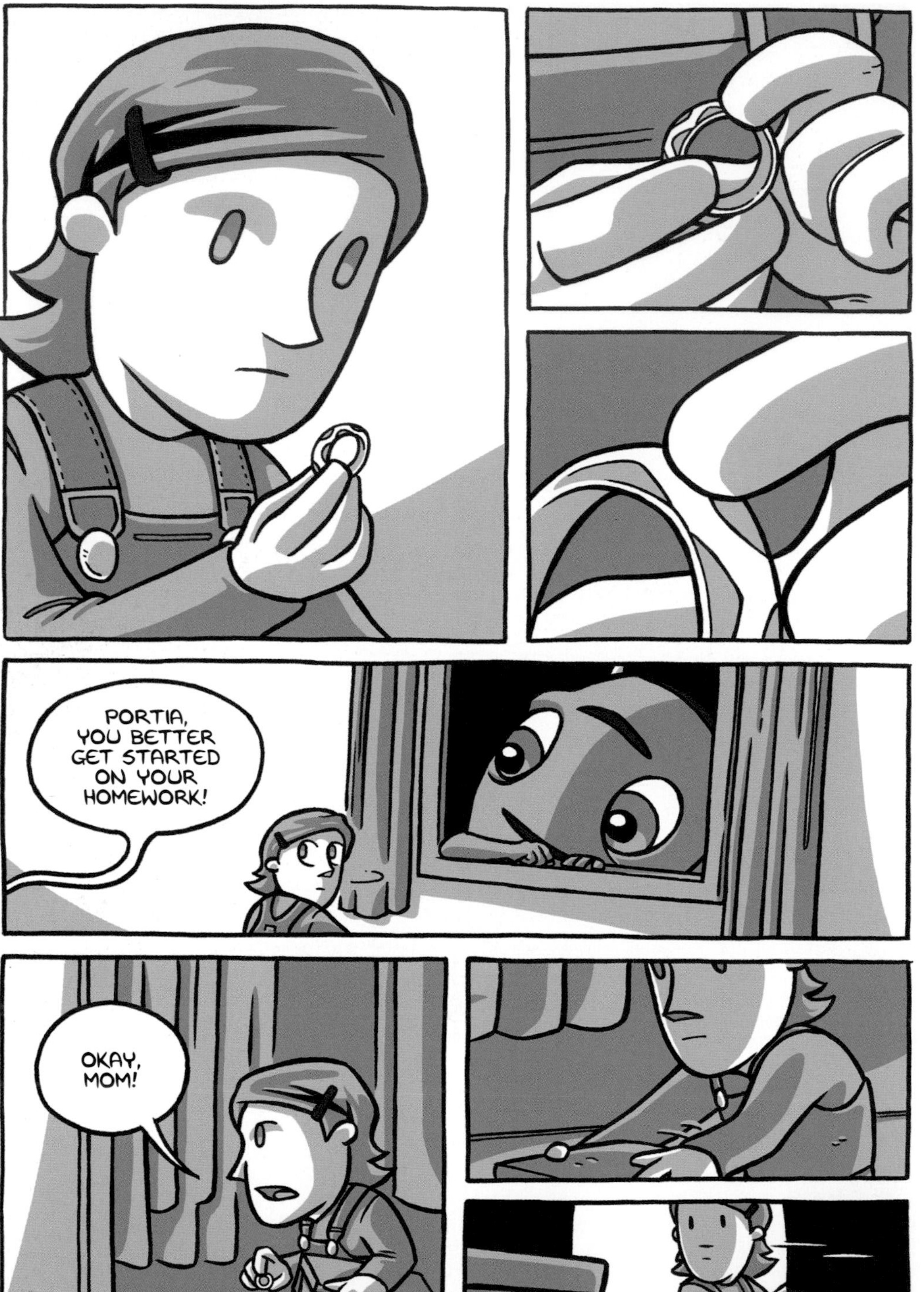
PORTIA, YOU BETTER GET STARTED ON YOUR HOMEWORK!
OKAY, MOM!

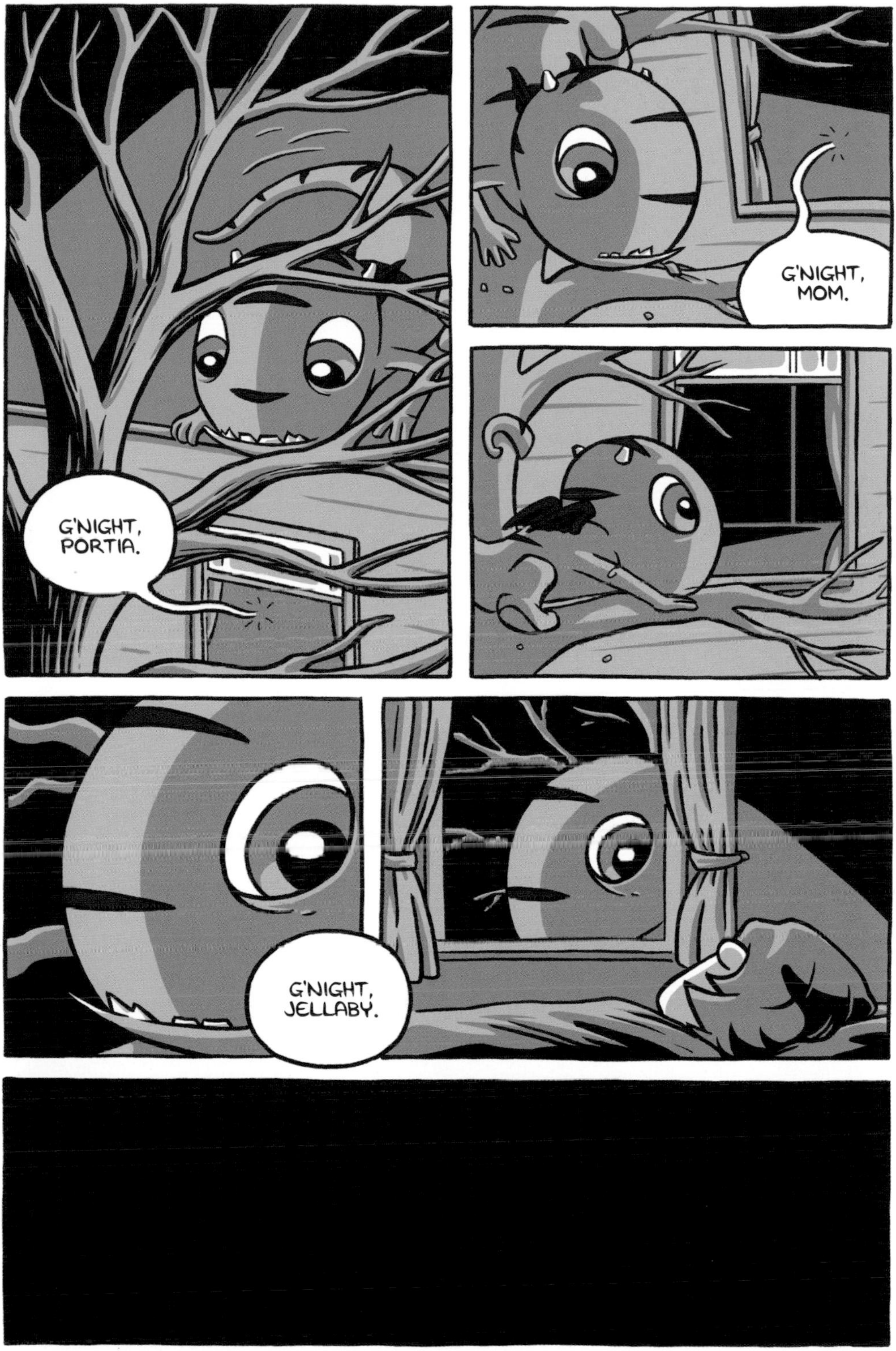
G'NIGHT, PORTIA.
G'NIGHT, MOM.
G'NIGHT, JELLABY.

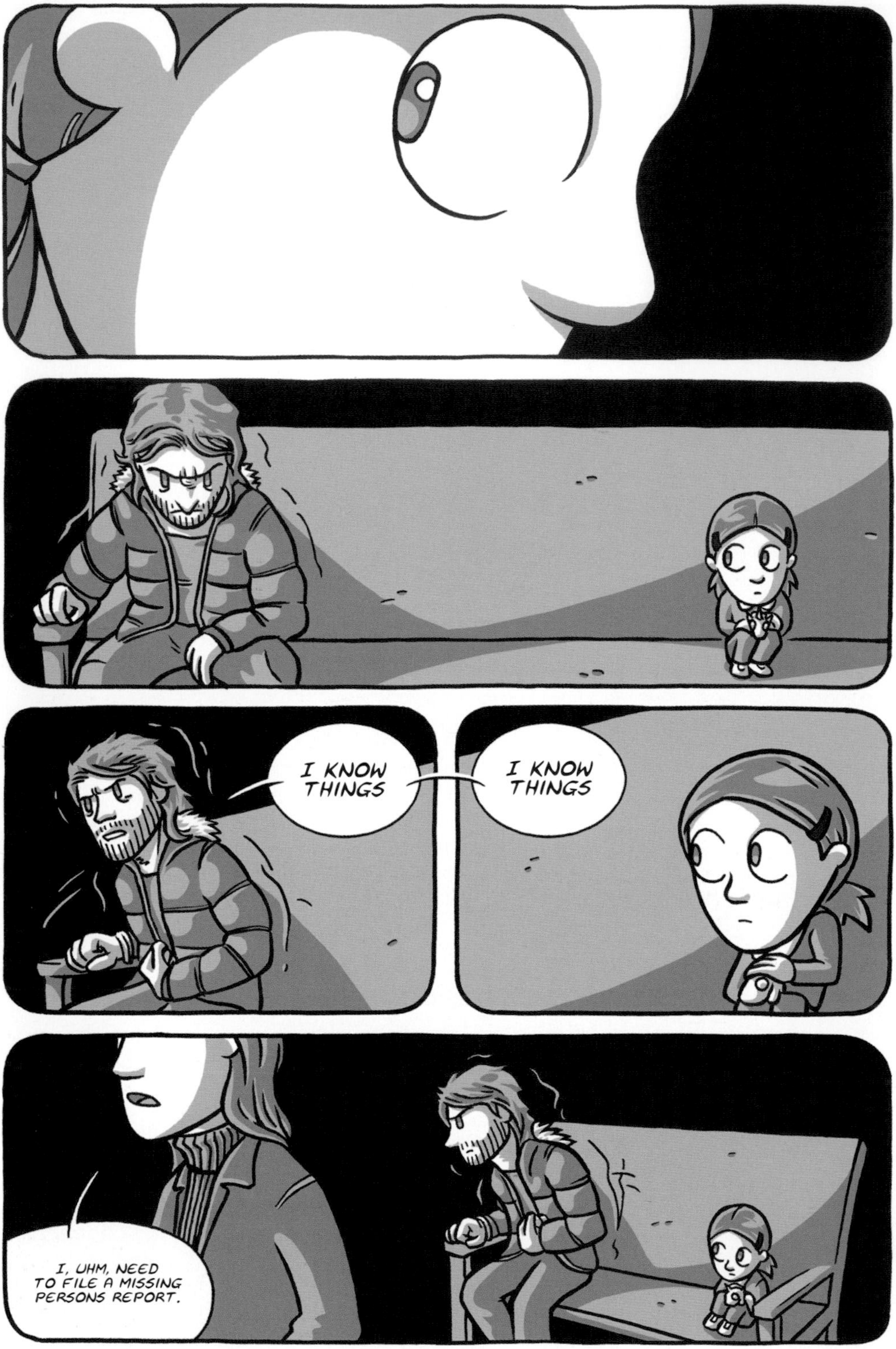
I KNOW THINGS
I KNOW THINGS
I, UHM, NEED TO FILE A MISSING PERSONS REPORT.

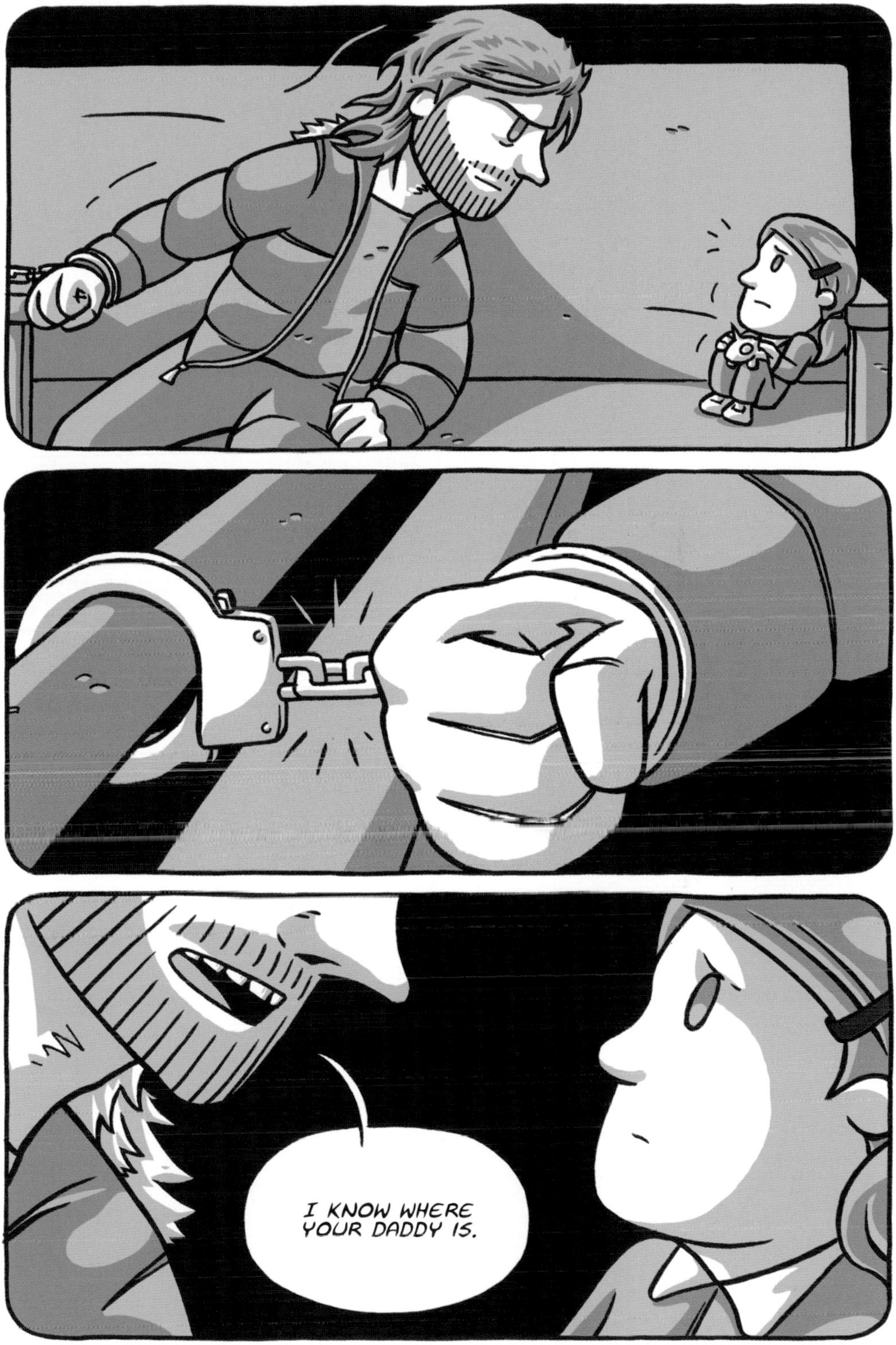
I KNOW WHERE YOUR DADDY IS.

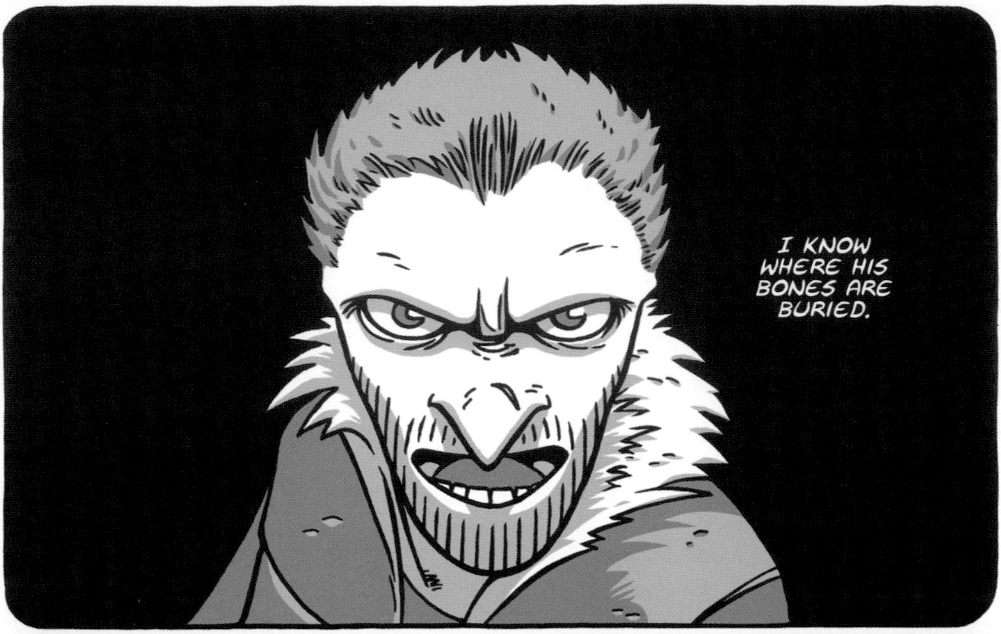
I KNOW WHERE HIS BONES ARE BURIED.

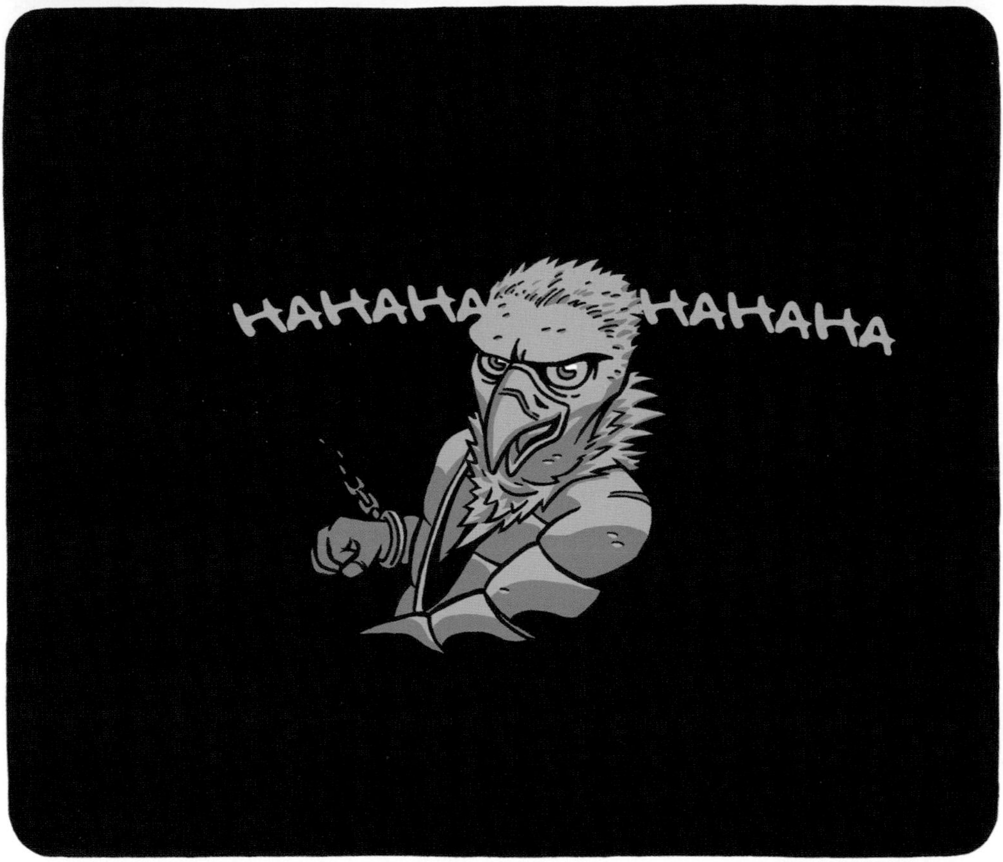
HAHAHA HAHAHA

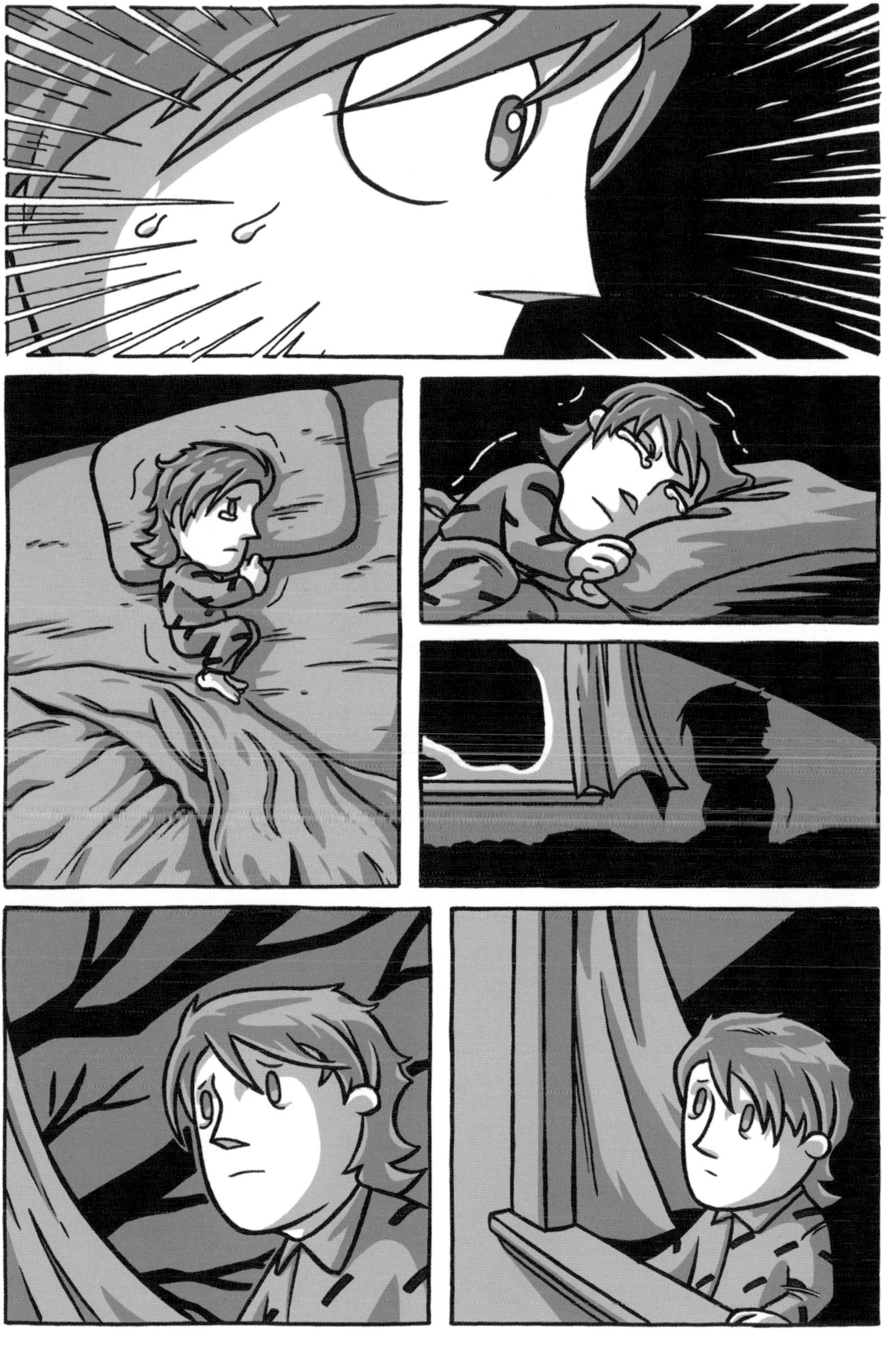

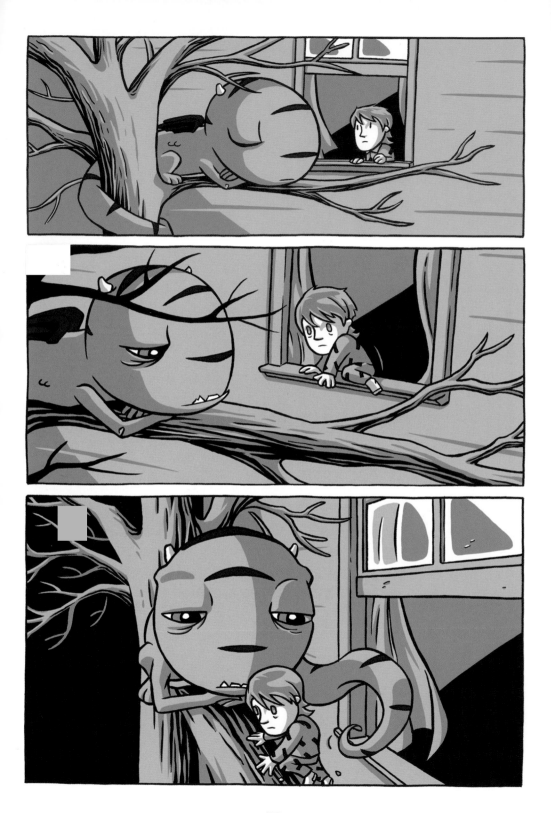

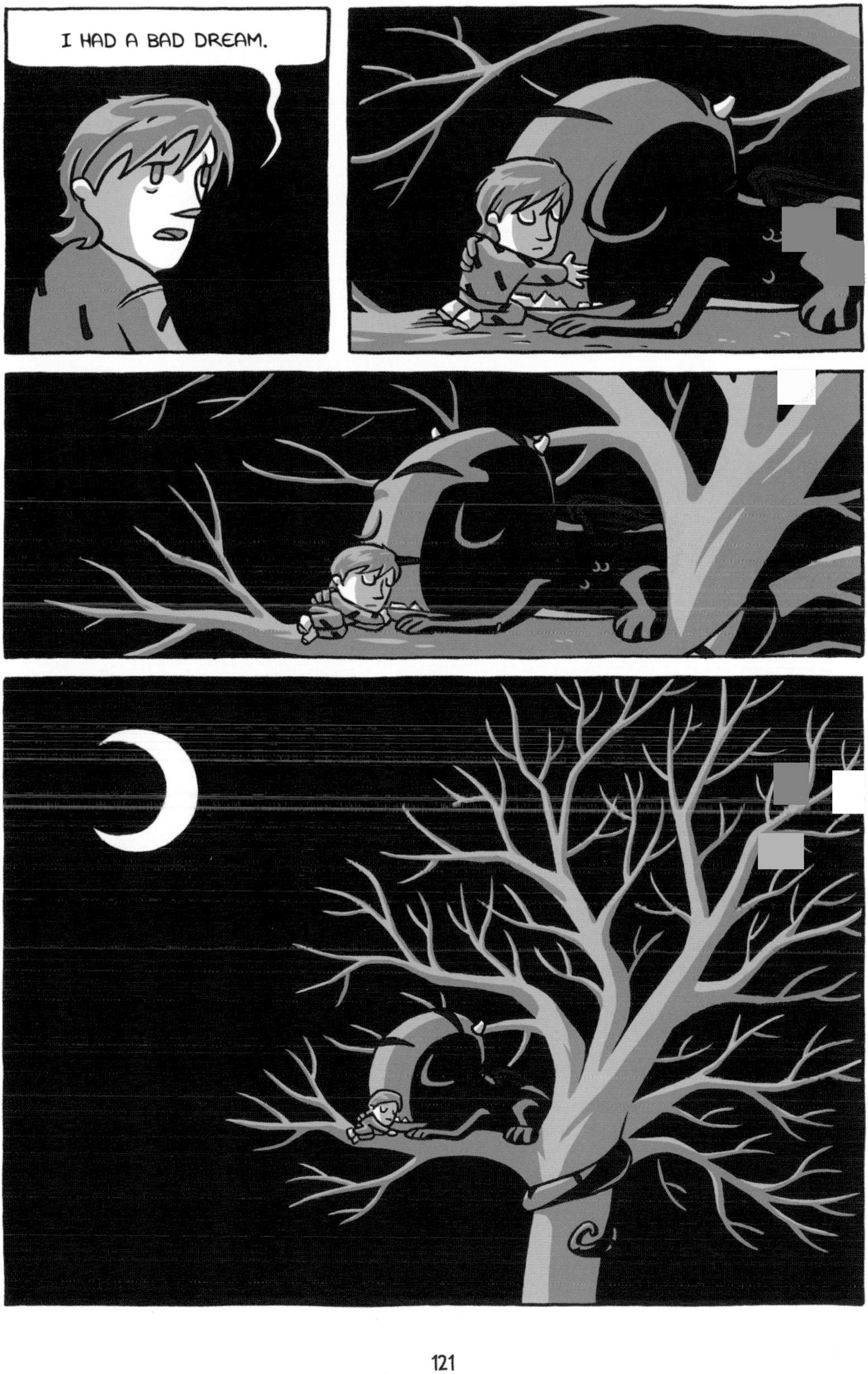
I HAD A BAD DREAM.

CHAPTER FIVE

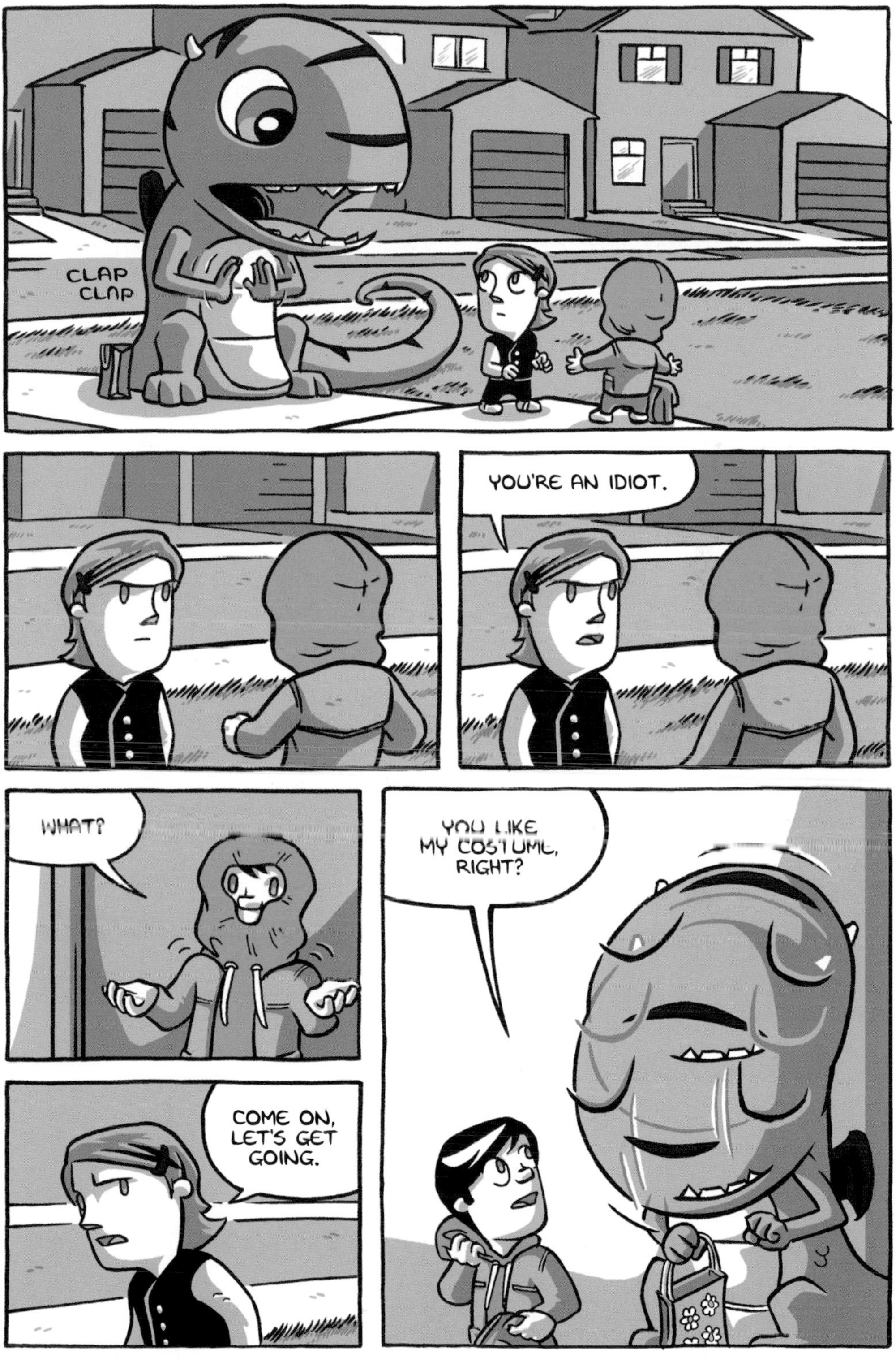
CLAP
CLAP
YOU'RE AN IDIOT.
WHAT?
YOU LIKE MY COSTUME, RIGHT?
COME ON, LET'S GET GOING.

127

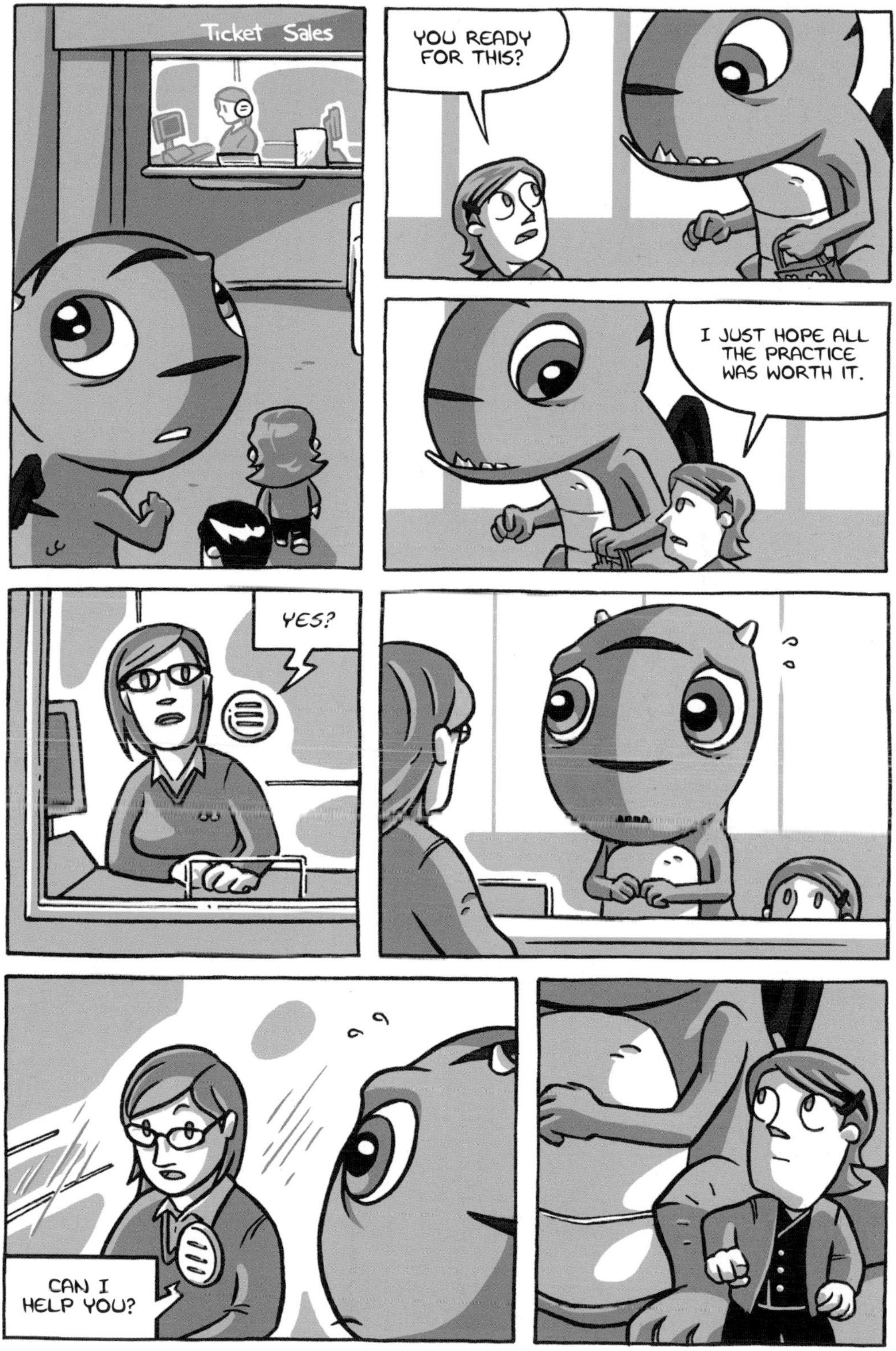
Ticket Sales
YOU READY FOR THIS?
I JUST HOPE ALL THE PRACTICE WAS WORTH IT.
YES?
CAN I HELP YOU?

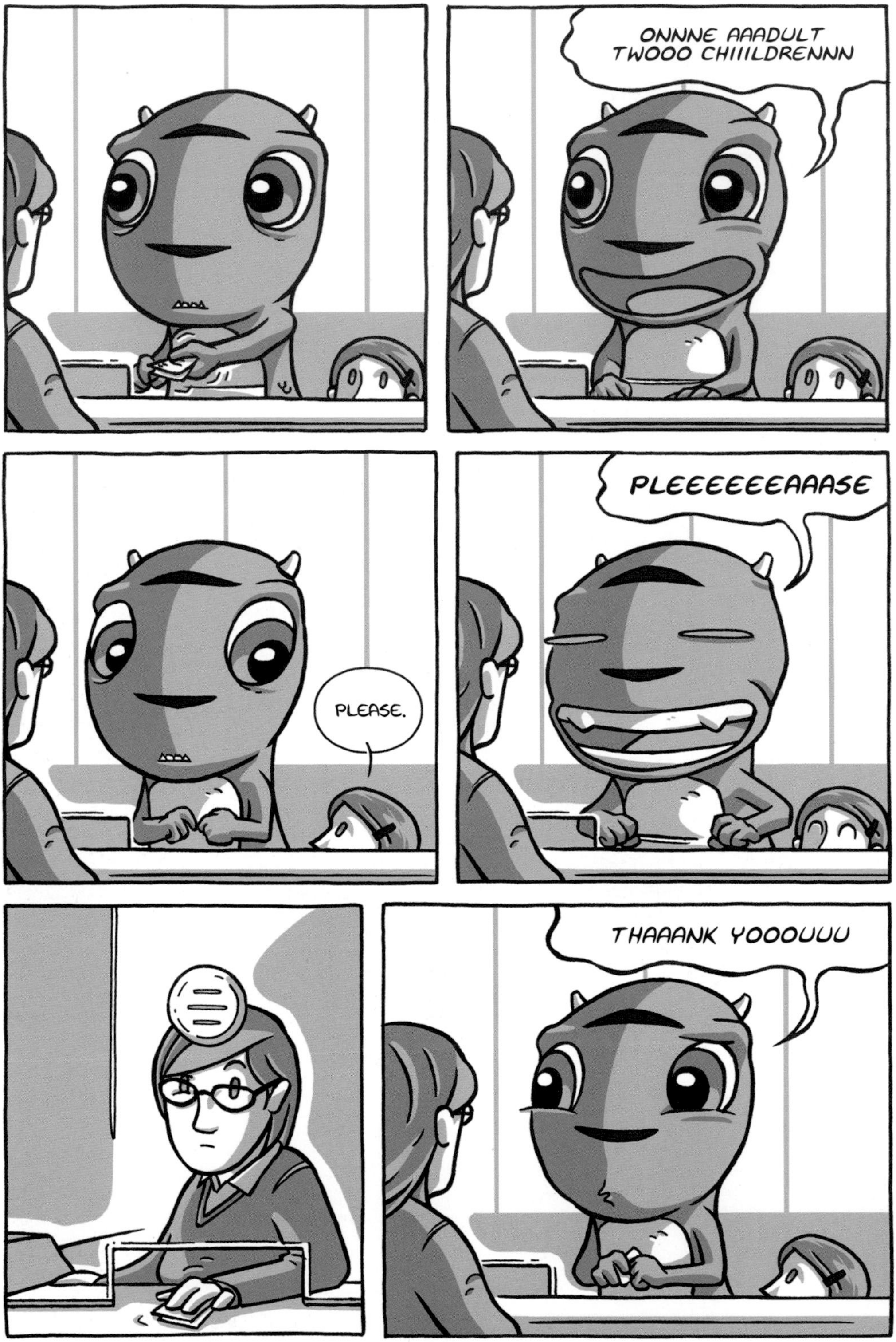
ONNNE AAADULT TWOOO CHIIILDRENNN
PLEASE.
PLEEEEEEEAAASE
THAAANK YOOOUUU

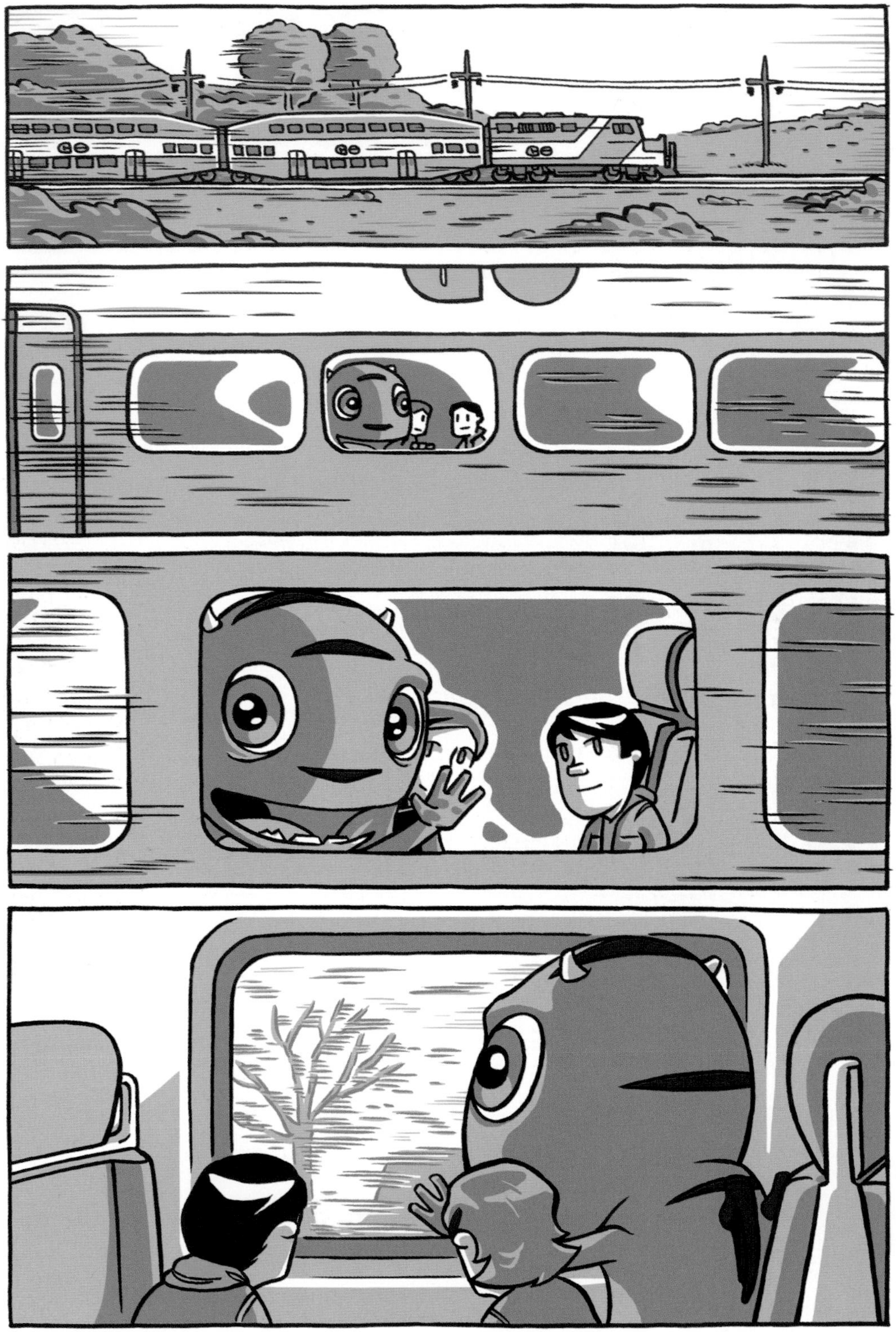

135

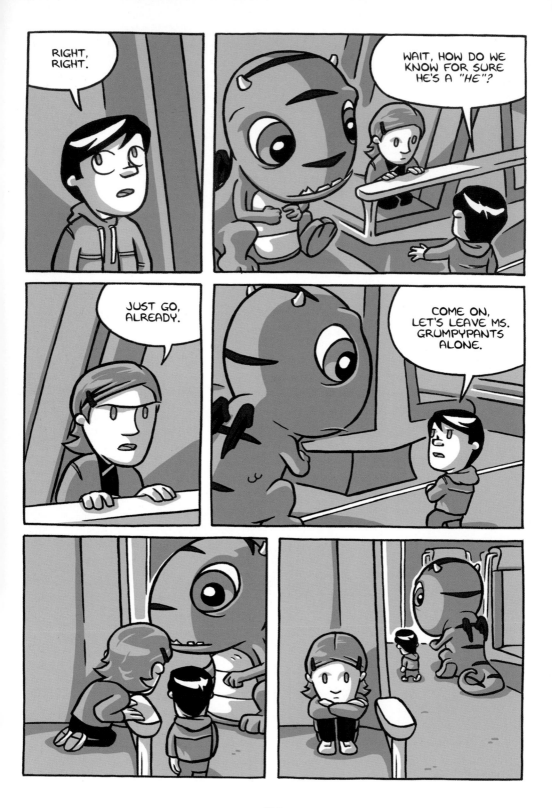

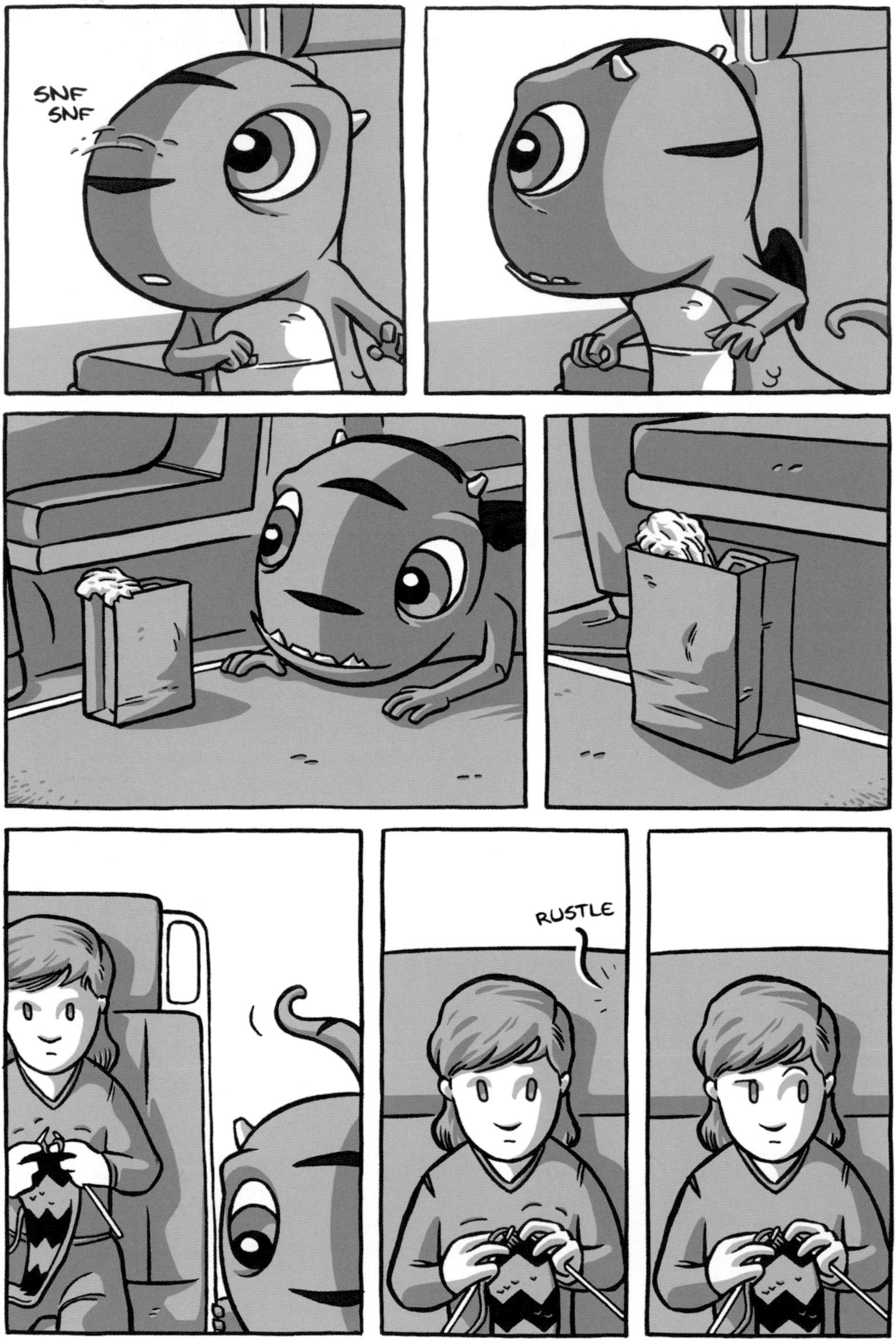
SNF
SNF
RUSTLE

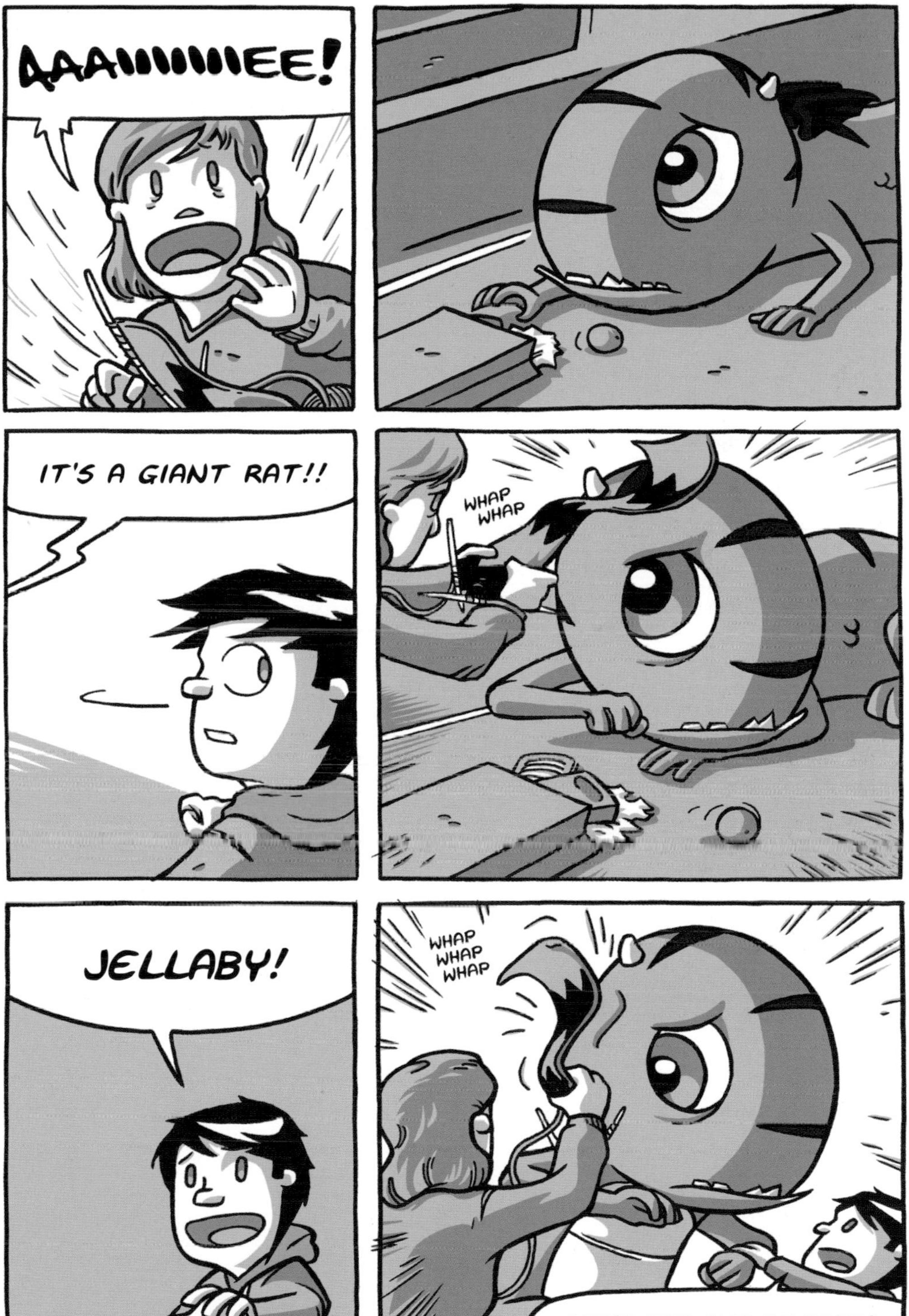
AAAIIIIIIIEE!
IT'S A GIANT RAT!!
WHAP WHAP
JELLABY!
WHAP WHAP WHAP
LET'S GET OUT OF HERE!

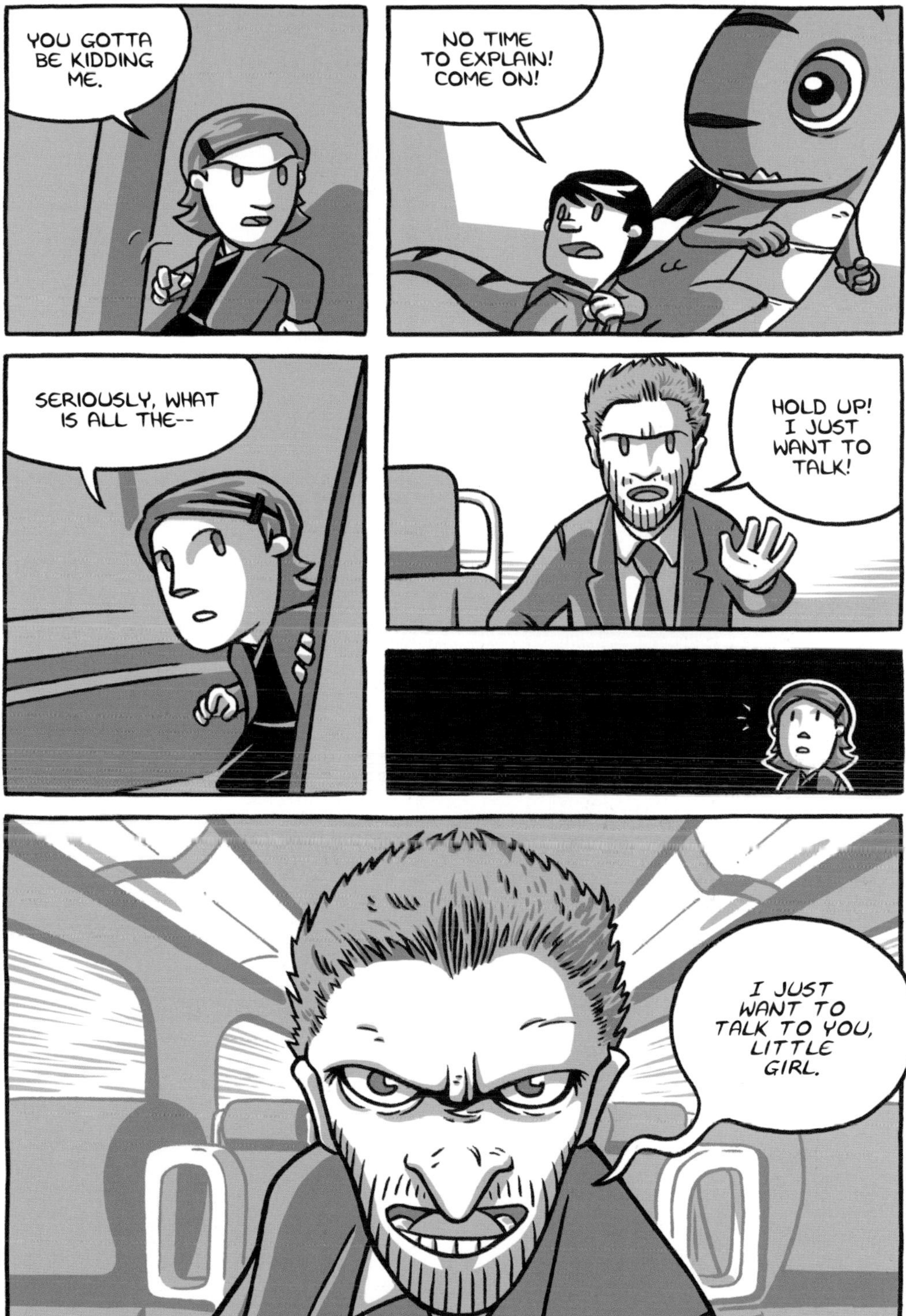
YOU GOTTA BE KIDDING ME.
NO TIME TO EXPLAIN! COME ON!
SERIOUSLY, WHAT IS ALL THE--
HOLD UP! I JUST WANT TO TALK!
I JUST WANT TO TALK TO YOU, LITTLE GIRL.

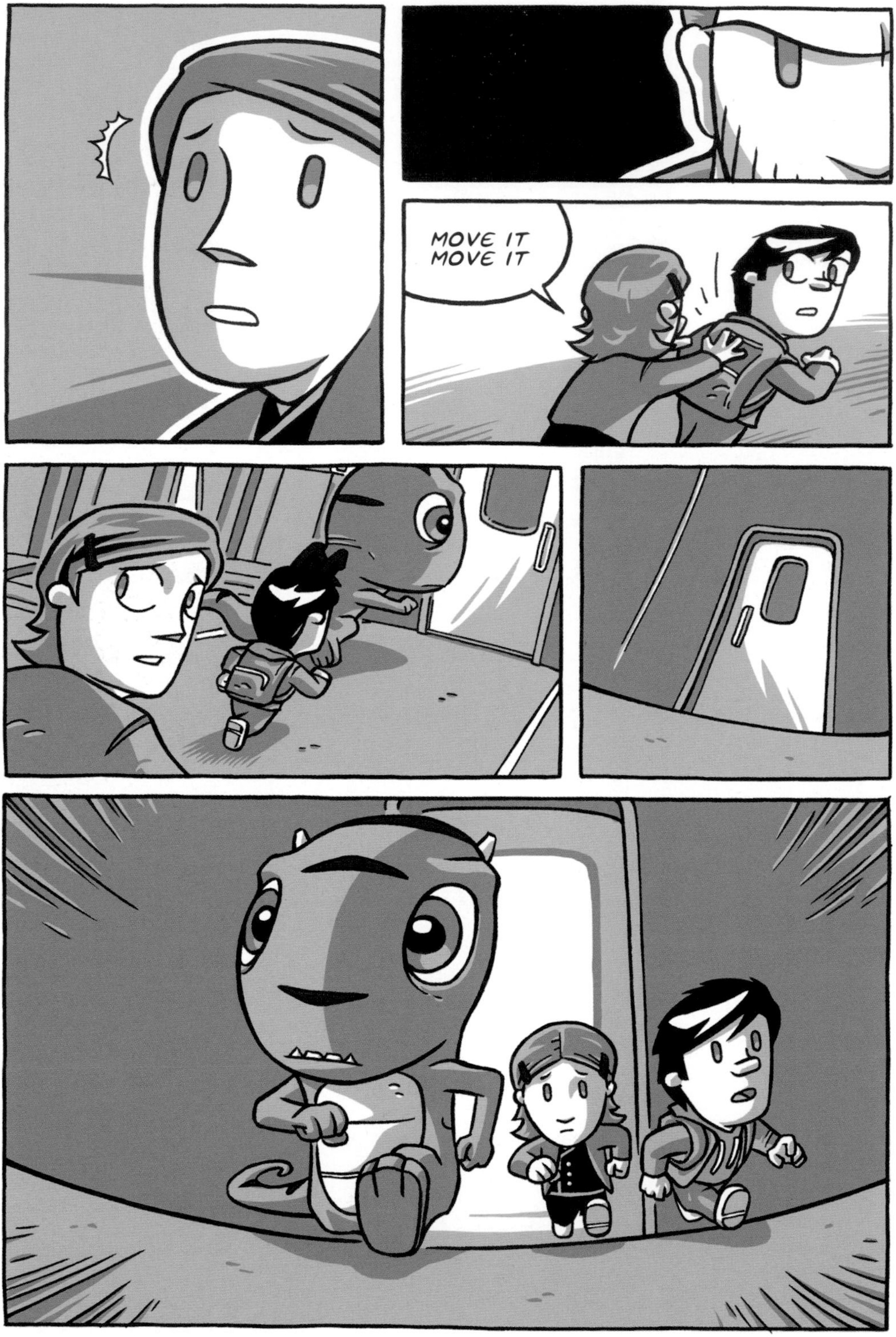
MOVE IT
MOVE IT

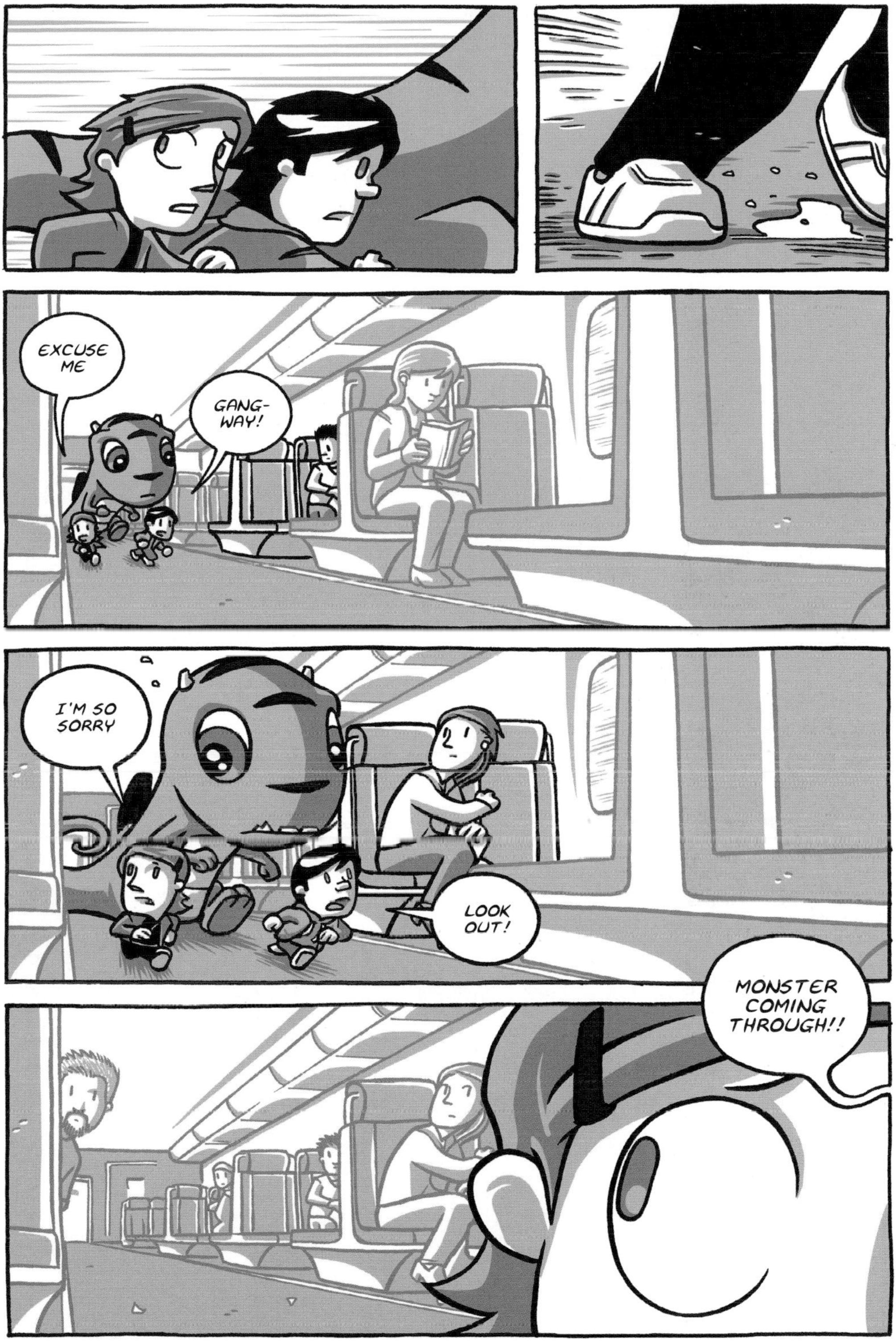
EXCUSE ME
GANG-WAY!
I'M SO SORRY
LOOK OUT!
MONSTER COMING THROUGH!!

146

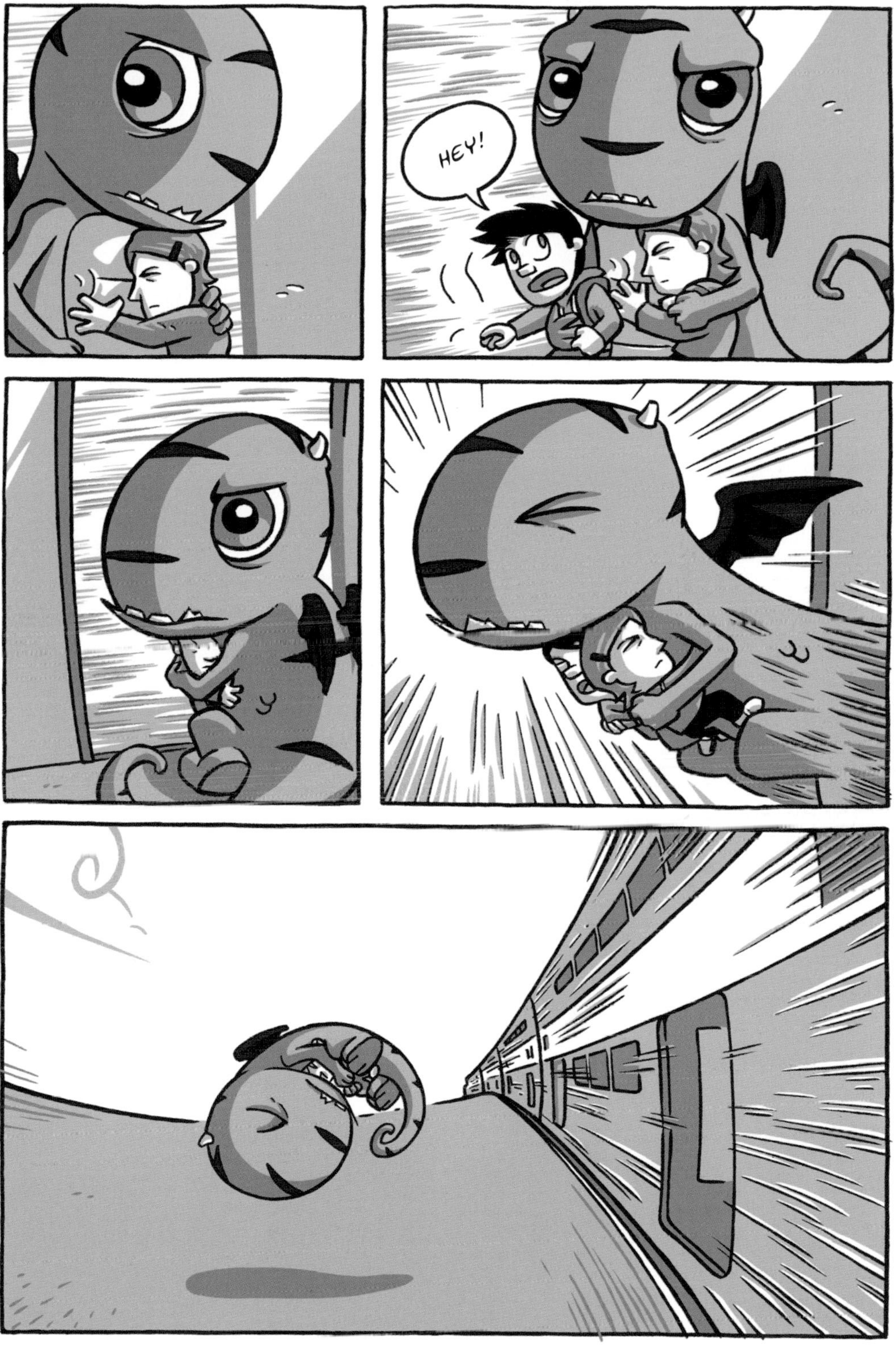
HEY!

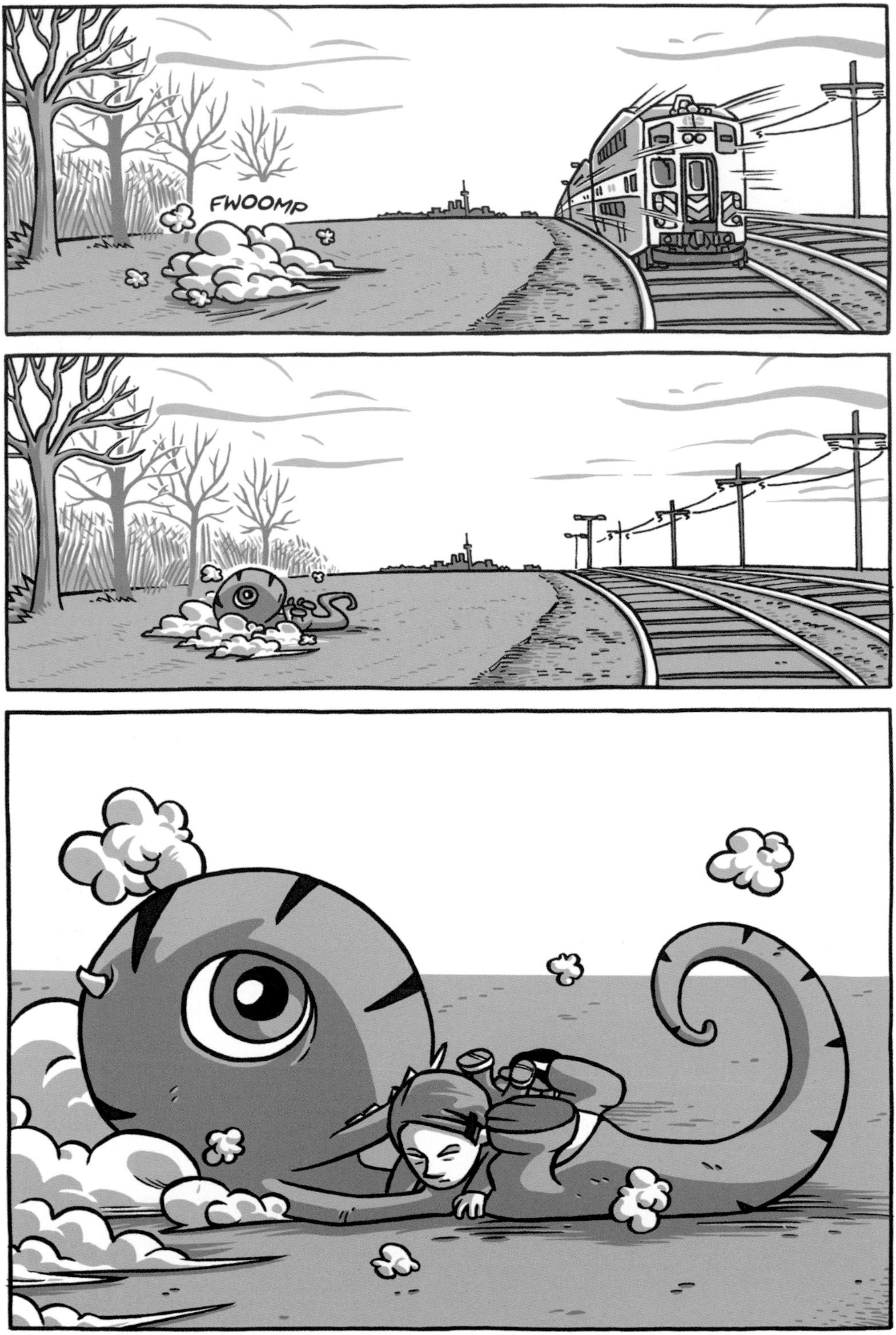
FWOOMP

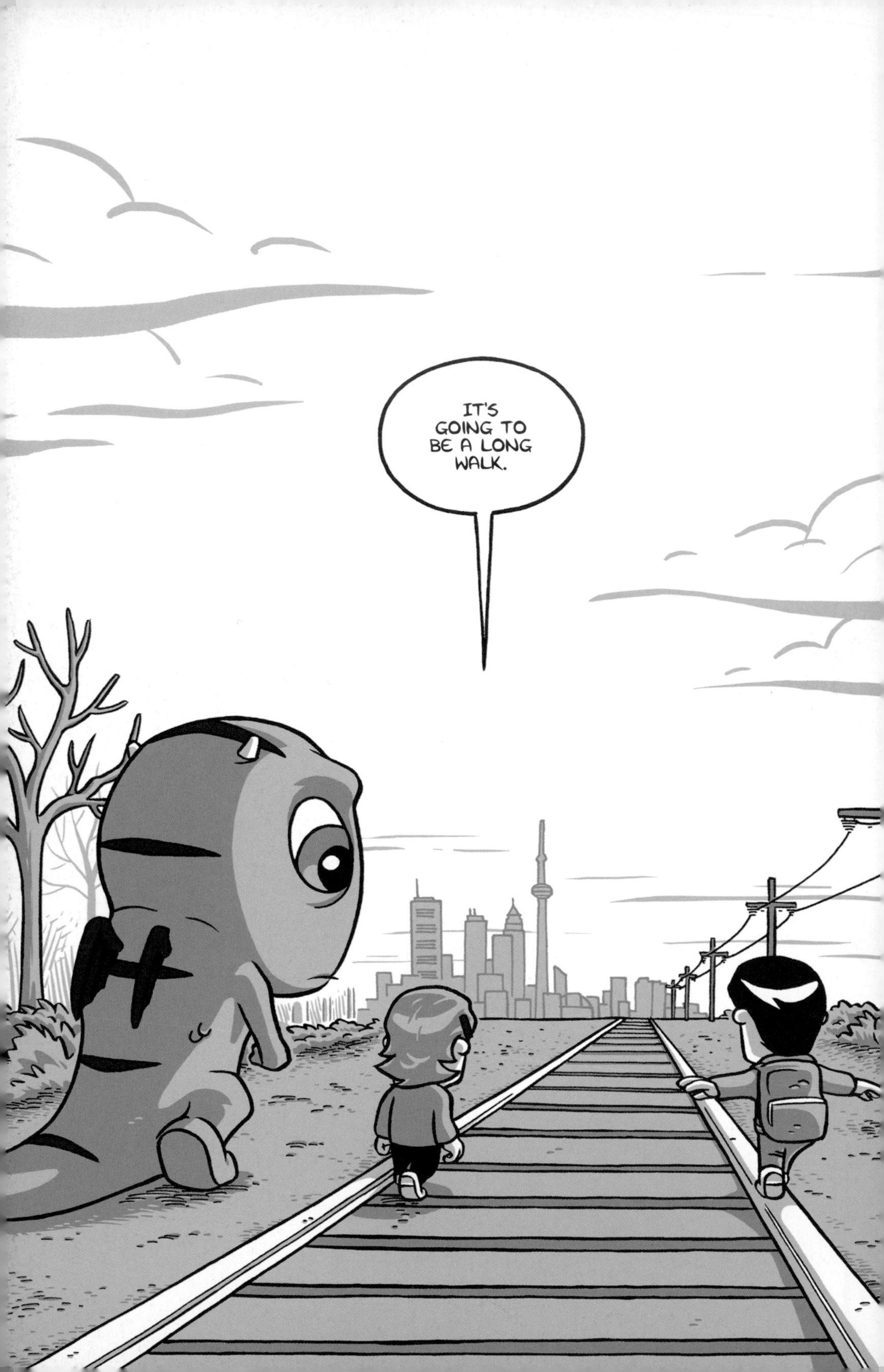
IT'S GOING TO BE A LONG WALK.

To be continued in...

Monster in the City

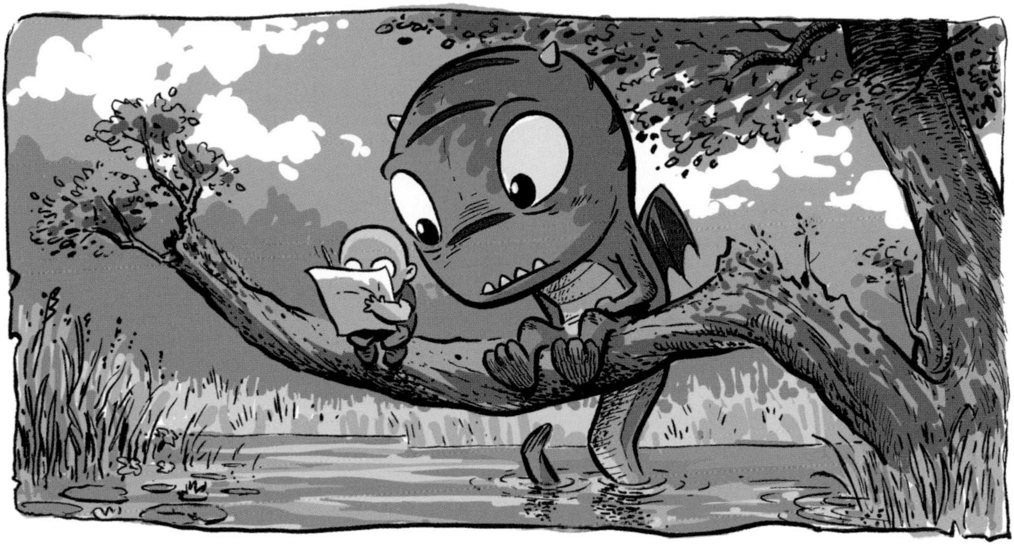

About the Author

Born in England and raised in Hong Kong, Kean Soo settled in Canada, where he planned to embark on a career in electrical engineering. However, he discovered that he'd rather draw comics instead. Kean began posting his comics on the Internet in 2002, and later became an assistant editor and regular contributor to the all-ages *Flight* anthologies. Kean was nominated for an Eisner Award and received a Joe Shuster Award for Best Comics for Kids for his work on *Jellaby*.

Kean likes carrots, but not nearly as much as he likes tuna sandwiches, usually with lots and lots of wasabi mayonnaise.

Portrait of the author by Phil Craven

Q&A with Kean Soo

Where did you get the idea for Jellaby?

The idea actually came from a single drawing in my sketchbook. At the time, I was trying to think of ideas for my first graphic novel, so in my sketchbook, I was just having fun drawing all the things I love to draw -- things like robots, monsters, and cars.

It was one of those drawings that really stood out to me: a little girl hugging a terrifying, grub-like monster. And because the monster was so terrifying, it made me wonder: why would these two be hugging each other? Why would they even be friends?

As I tried to answer these questions, it started raising more questions, and I wanted to find out more about these two. From there, the characters of Portia and Jellaby started to take shape, and the story naturally spun out of that.

Above: The very first drawing of Portia and Jellaby. I had originally named the monster Cuddles, mostly because at the time, I thought it was a funny name for such a terrifying monster.

Why did you choose pink and purple for the colors of the book?

I had originally designed the book to be printed in black and white, but when I first started drawing Jellaby, I didn't have a publisher and I was just posting the pages online. Because it didn't cost anything extra to post color pages to the web, I decided to use pink and purple to make the pages a little more interesting, but those colors were also chosen because they could be easily converted back to black and white when the book was printed.

When a publisher did get in touch with me about printing the book, they liked the pink and purple colors so much that we ended up keeping them anyway!

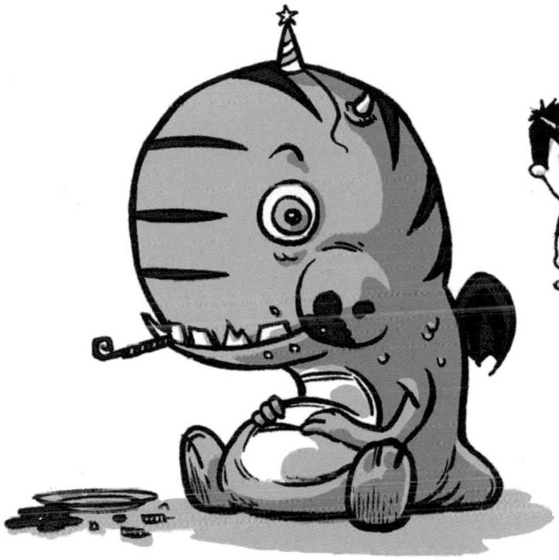

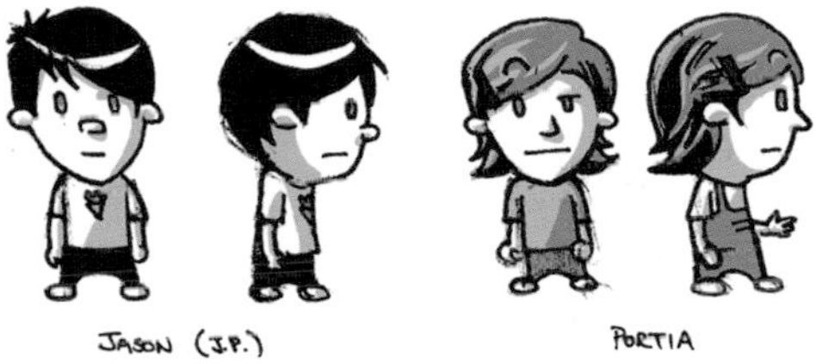
JASON (J.P.)
PORTIA

Above: The first color tests for the Jellaby characters.

What do you use to draw Jellaby?

I write and lay out my pages in my sketchbook with a regular HB pencil. I use that same pencil to draw the pages full size on 9" x 12" smooth bristol board, and I ink over top of those pencils using a Kuretake brush pen and Micron technical pens for smaller details. The finished pages are then scanned into a computer, where I letter and color the pages digitally.

How long have you been drawing for? When did you start drawing comics?

I've been drawing for as long as I can remember -- I specifically remember when I was around 4 years old, after watching the movie *Tron*, I would draw pages upon pages of light cycle battles. I didn't start making comics until I was much older, but I found that drawing a daily webcomic for almost two years really taught me a lot. In fact, I was still learning new tricks and techniques even while I was working on *Jellaby*.

Sketches

FIRST DAY OF SCHOOL

SHOOF SHOOF SHOOF

Above: More early sketches of Portia and Jellaby. Some of these sketches eventually made it into the final book (compare the sketch on the top right with Chapter Five's opening page).

Left: Sometimes I love a scene so much, I enjoy revisiting it when I'm warming up to draw. Here's another interpretation of Portia and Jellaby "shoofing" through the leaves from Chapter Two.